THE RAIN MENDER

© Copyright 2022- Kathleen T.N. Smith

All rights reserved. Permission is granted to copy or reprint portions for any noncommercial use, except they may not be posted online without permission.

Wyatt House books may be ordered through booksellers or by contacting:

WYATT HOUSE PUBLISHING
399 Lakeview Dr. W.
Mobile, Alabama 36695
www.wyattpublishing.com
editor@wyattpublishing.com

Because of the dynamic nature of the Internet, any web address or links contained in this book may have changed since publication and may no longer be valid.

Cover design by: Mariah Nystrom Hayes

Author photo by Amanda Smith/Hamilton Rose Photography

Interior design by: Mark Wyatt

ISBN 13:978-1-954798-07-6

Printed in the United States of America

THE RAIN MENDER

BY
KATHLEEN T.N. SMITH

Wyatt House Publishing

Mobile, Alabama

DEDICATION

To the One who saves. May He touch the hearts
and lives of all who seek Him.

HENRY

The old man sat silently staring out across the dark mountain lake. The still waters were a reflection of the quiet emptiness that had been plaguing him all day. As incomplete thoughts flickered like elusive fireflies, darting in and out of his troubled mind, he couldn't help but to reflect on the past.

He always turned to the front porch of the house that his father had built to do his best thinking. Today, he was finding it impossible to put a finger on what was truly bothering him. If only he could have five more minutes with his dad. He just wished he would have taken the time to listen more closely to his words of wisdom when he had the chance. There were so many questions yet to be answered.

A slight breeze lifted the collar of his well-worn shirt. He could almost feel his father's hand resting on his shoulder as memories from days gone by came flooding back to mind. Sweet memories, that gently calmed his nerves and brought a smile to his weathered face.

"Son, look out over the lake. This is where we belong. When the good Lord takes me to the great by and by, there will still be time spent here with your son and grandson. And they too, will come to know that this is where they belong..."

His father was right. Henry had raised his own son on the lake, and watching him grow from a small boy to a strong man was a gift he would always treasure. When a tragic car accident took his son before his time, Henry learned quickly that life can change in the blink of an eye. Then, when his daughter, Stella, had a baby boy and chose to leave him behind on Henry's doorstep, he would come to realize the importance of his young grandson's presence in his life. So many memories...

Henry was pulled back to the present when a deep, throbbing ache in his lower back materialized. He knew that his time was limited on this earth and he shivered when a black feeling of foreboding cast a shadow over him. He hadn't noticed that the wind was beginning to pick up and he had only to look up to see that a storm was coming. His mind momentarily cleared with the coming of it, but the ache in his back only intensified. Arthritis and an old work injury were a dual barometer when it came to changes in the weather. He knew that the approaching storm was coming in fast. He could feel it in his bones.

"Batten down the hatch!" he said with conviction to himself. First, he had to secure the old wooden chair he'd been sitting on. If not, it was sure to be reduced to kindling when it blew off the porch. It was definitely on its last leg, just like him.

"Heave-ho, against the house you go!" The chair was too bulky for him to lift so he would just have to wedge it into the corner as best he could. Next, the storm shutters would need to be latched over the windows. Climbing up on a ladder was out of the question, so he'd just have to wait for Jake to come home to handle that task. His young, strong Jacob. The blessing that his father predicted was to be a part of his life, was the reason his heart continued to beat.

The wind, steadily building into a frenzy, caused the nearby trees to dance wildly to its powerful song, while a small frog at the water's edge jumped into the churning black body of water.

Henry noticed, when he happened to glance up, that the tumultuous clouds over Mount Chloe were rapidly heading in his direction. This was not good. The mournful cry from an eagle battling its way across Pale Moon Lake was also an omen of what was to come.

The old man stood clinging to the sturdy porch railing, contemplating his next move. The howling wind was disorienting and it made keeping his balance a struggle. It was a relatively short distance from where he was standing to the door, but it was proving to be no simple task getting there. He lunged towards the doorknob when a ferocious gust threatened to topple him over. If not for a strong pair of hands reaching out to steady him, he certainly would have fallen.

"*Gramps!* What are you doing outside?! Haven't you been listening to the weather report on the radio?! What's coming can lift you up and carry you to the next county! Let's get you inside!"

Jake, his handsome young grandson wearing a letterman's jacket, showed up just in the nick of time. Together, they fought their way into the house and Jake kicked the door shut behind them with his foot. Thunder boomed loudly, followed by a blinding flash of lightning, and Henry Davis was grateful to be safely indoors.

JACOB

Henry Davis was Jacob's best friend. After all, his gramps was the one to give him a safe place to call home when his mother decided that her dreams were more important than raising a son. Jacob's father had never been a part of the picture, and he never would be. He left for parts unknown before the baby was ever born, and when Stella left the small boy on her father's doorstep, everything in life changed... for all of them.

No doubt about it, those early years were rough. Life on Pale Moon Lake became the healing balm to soothe the young boy's aching heart, and as he grew older, the young man was more determined than ever to be someone that didn't let Henry Davis down.

When the small boy first arrived in Chloe, he was quiet and shy. On his first day of kindergarten, Jacob cried when Henry walked away after handing him over to his teacher. Abandonment was a harsh lesson in life. One, that clearly, had an effect on the little boy.

After the tears subsided, Jake slowly ventured out onto the playground and Maxwell Darington came crashing into his world. Max, literally, collided with Jake near the jungle gym, and when the offender pulled his victim up off the ground, he said, "I'm Max, and you're my best friend."

As far as buddies were concerned, those words spoken on the kindergarten playground proved prophetic, and all through elementary, middle and high school, the two remained fast friends.

While Jake lived at the lake with his grandfather, Max grew up in a luxurious home with his parents, sister, and their pet dog. A real family. Henry, happy to see his grandson flourish, was forever grateful for the love that they shared with Jacob. Over the years, despite circumstances surrounding his humble beginnings, Jacob was able to experience family life with the Darington's.

In high school, football turned out to be the perfect outlet for Jake. He felt honored when chosen to be team captain, and the responsibility of setting a positive example for his teammates was easily embraced. He'd been the star quarterback for three of his four years with the team, and he worked hard at encouraging others while honing his skills. More than anything though, he just wanted to make his grandfather proud.

When Jacob entered his teenage years, a glimpse of the man that he would one day become, reflected in his grandfather's eyes.

School was done for the day, and football practice had just ended, when Jake heard the news that the weather would soon be taking a turn for the worse. He grabbed his backpack and keys and ran to his truck, knowing that his grandfather would need help around the house before the storm's arrival.

WALLACE

"Noooooooooo, Wallace! Has your brain left your skull?!" The agitated girl sitting across from him in the empty science lab annoyingly tapped her pencil on the desk.

"My dear, sweet Daisy... I don't see that there are any other viable options. I have done my research and reached the only obvious conclusion. To embody higher learning, one must strive for excellence... and that, my dear, is what I have done. The scientific study of nature, in its predictable and unpredictable state, is precisely what we will be attempting to understand. The Senior Class trip will provide the perfect opportunity for us to achieve the ultimate goal. *Enlightenment!*"

"For crying out loud, Wallace. It's just a mandatory trek for seniors into the great outdoors. It's a glorified camping trip! And those of us blessed with less *hard-drive* tend to see it as an opportunity to sneak cigarettes and alcohol under the noses of our unsuspecting teachers. It's also a time for our parents to pour a cocktail of their own as they thank the Higher Power for a week without us. It's a time for everyone, Wallace!"

"But Daisy... what about collecting specimens? Rare beetles and insects? Plant life... soil samples... air samples?! You know, it's a lot fresher the higher up you go."

"Wallace. You... and maybe even I... may see a need for expanding our horizons via higher learning, but the majority of our classmates are online as we speak, finding out how to make *moonshine* in seven days or less. Therefore, you can bring your plastic collection organizer and your high-tech butterfly net, but I'm limiting myself to a journal and a pen and the *only* scientific experiment that I will personally be conducting... thanks to our ingenious school chums... will be... 'Is the taste for moonshine a given, or an acquired thing?' College will be starting soon enough and I'll worry about my potential lack of intelligence then!"

Daisy threw her notebook and pencil into her backpack, tossed the strap over her shoulder and marched out of the classroom, slamming the door in her wake.

Wallace stared after her in amazement. "Women!"

Turning to Slim, the skeletal science lab mascot, he said, "... but isn't she just about the most endearing thing to ever grace planet Earth?"

With that thought in mind, Wallace turned on his laptop and searched the web for *Portable Distilleries*. At the very least, he could conduct a private study on alcohol content and its effect on his gorgeous, charming, funny, adorable classmate named Daisy. She was worth furthering his research.

Wallace T. Kramer was a scientific genius in his own mind. With a little hard work and perseverance, he was certain he could produce a recipe for the perfect love potion. Yes, Wallace was determined to give Daisy Wilson something to write about in that journal of hers!

MAXWELL

Max was careful to place his soft drink can on the white leather coaster that was sitting on the *$8,000.00 coffee table.*

The house rules were as follows*: No feet on the table. No glasses or drinks on the table. If it spills... you're done! No food, no books, no backpacks and no car keys on the beloved table.* According to their mother, he and Caroline would be better off staying ten feet from it at all times. In his mind, this was no way to live.

Max dreamed of owning his own place one day. Furniture to be lived on. That's what his house would be furnished with. Better yet, a boat on the water would be more like it. Possibly a sleek design of his own making.

He oftentimes found himself in the midst of a daydream. Max pictured himself living an exciting life on a lake or more possibly an ocean. Unhindered by parental rules and regulations, he would be free to explore. His sailing vessel would be made from solid wood and adorned with crisp white sails. True craftsmanship! Something to admire and be proud of.

If the ocean was to be his destiny, he would travel the seas and keep a journal of all of his adventures. Then, when he was too old for the seafaring lifestyle, he'd find a reputable publisher and share his life's story with fellow dreamers and sailors.

Dreaming of a future of his own making, disappeared when his dog, *Trainwreck*, almost knocked his drink off the table with his tail on his way up onto the couch.

"Trainwreck!! Where did you come from? I thought you were at the Dog Spa having your nails clipped and your mangy coat groomed!" Obviously, he hadn't made it to the groomers as his thick chocolate brown coat was covered with leaves and twigs.

"Mom's really going to love this! Down, boy! Let's get you back outside."

As Max escorted the dog to the back door, he noticed that dark clouds were brewing in the distance. After Trainwreck was back in his element, Max headed to the kitchen for a bag of potato chips.

Returning to the living room, he reached for the remote to flip on the TV. Next, he ripped open the chips, kicked his feet up on the coffee table, and proceeded to munch. Life was a lot simpler when his mom was away, shopping in New York.

The Weather Alert flashed across the screen, interrupting his favorite television show.

"Stay indoors! If on the road seek shelter immediately! A severe storm is heading towards the town of Chloe... I repeat... a severe storm is heading towards the town of Chloe!"

Max clicked off the TV, tossed the remote onto the coffee table, followed by the opened bag of chips. In all honesty, Max loved his parents, even though there seemed to be a lot of rules to follow. His mom and dad had always been there for him, and he felt obligated to be there for them. In his head, he could hear his mother's voice all the way from New York City. Accustomed to the drill, he headed for the door while his mother's voice replayed her instructions...

"Maxwell... it is your responsibility to make sure things are secured outside the house when bad weather comes our way. Your father is a very busy man and frankly, is seldom at home. We all must do our part here, son!"

The question was... where was his sister, Caroline? She should be home to help as well. Truth be known, he'd be glad when he could move out after graduation.

As he stepped out the back, he was startled when the wind slammed the door shut behind him.

"Wow! This one's going to be a doozie!"

He ran against the whipping wind, grabbing flying lawn chairs and small flower pots along the way.

CLAIRE

"Hurry up, Annie!" Franklin grabbed his little sister's hand, dragging her along behind him. "Claire! Wait up!"

As the three siblings trudged along the sidewalk, the exasperated young boy loudly exclaimed, "Sisters! What were you thinking, God? Why not brothers?!"

"That's not a very nice thing to say, Franklin..." sniffled the tired little girl in tow.

When they reached Mathews Hardware Store, their father's business, all three tried to shove their way through the door at the same time while the bell overhead chimed twice, announcing their arrival.

"Daddy!" cried Annie, as she raced into her father's outstretched arms. "Franklin's being mean again and I think I need an ice cream cone today!"

Fred Mathews looked forward to this hour each day. He was always eager to hear about what his children had learned in school, but mostly he was just happy to see their bright smiling faces. Especially, his little Annie's grin!

Annie was a bubbly little cherub, rosy cheeked, precocious, and known to daydream. She more often than not had a story to tell, and Franklin was readily available to tease her. *Annie Land*, reigned in that faraway place where imagination bloomed on treetops. A place where Princess Annie was in charge of picking prized blossoms. A Kingdom, where boys were seldom allowed to enter. Franklin was occasionally invited in. It really all depended on the day. Today, it appeared that he was on the outside looking in!

Imagination was in great supply within the Mathews family and it could be traced all the way back to Great, Great Granny Allie Mae Mathews. The original dreamer.

Franklin, a miniature version of his father, was at times more serious, and definitely a history buff. He pictured himself racing across the prairie, riding horses for the Pony Express. Blue jeans, a cowboy hat and boots were his preferred attire... and sisters were perfect for practicing roping skills on. Fred had to limit Franklin's time spent with his lasso... for obvious reasons.

Claire, his eldest daughter, was the quiet dreamer. She was a studious senior at Chloe High and tended to retreat into the shadows when around her peers. Painfully shy, her father Fred was forever trying to encourage his daughter to share her gift with those around her. She was an avid reader, wrote beautiful stories and poems, and song lyrics flowed freely from the end of her pen.

Fred knew that he'd have his work cut out for him when he was called into the school office for a conference. Apparently, there were a few kids in the school who teased and bullied Claire, calling her "*Minnie*," the quiet little mouse! They tried tripping her in the hall and enjoyed slamming her locker when she had only just opened it. Kids were mean, no doubt about it.

Claire's mother understood her best. Stacy Mathews was a kindergarten teacher and she was well aware of childhood antics.

The harmless ones... and the not so harmless ones.

As Claire watched her father swing Annie around in the store, she wished she could be little again. Maybe she'd have a second chance at being courageous, and then she could escape her invisibility. She didn't feel the need to stand center stage with a bright light shining down upon her... but it might be nice to laugh along with the others when those standing in the light delivered comedic lines. Or maybe, just to have a best friend that she could share her secrets with.

She did have Dr. Morton Mathews in her life. Her toy poodle. A best friend, though pathetic, really. Looking on the brightside... he truly was a great listener. He loved to hear her sing songs and tell stories. If he were human, she was sure that he would be a doctor of psychology and would have the cure for her invisibility. After all, she was convinced that it would take a professional to provide the cure. Hopefully, one day...

"Claire, please take your brother and sister to the car. I'm going to lock up early today. Hal Clemmons just left and he said that the weatherman said that there's an incredibly powerful thunderstorm heading our way. It would be best if we beat it home. I talked to your mother and she's on her way to the house right now. I'll be done here in just a few minutes."

Claire nodded obediently and started for the door, grabbing Annie's hand on the way out.

"Aren't you going to hold my hand too, Claire?" teased Franklin. Claire glared at him over her shoulder and kept on walking. She honestly wouldn't mind if her invisibility worked on Franklin.

A brother... what was God thinking? Claire would have to address this problem with Dr. Mathews when she got home.

SHAYNE

Shayne could not believe her good fortune. The stars were shining down on her. Her parents were flying to Europe for twenty-two glorious days and she didn't have to go with them this time. A teenager's dream come true! At eighteen, she was very capable of taking care of herself. And wasn't it a shame that her grandparents were on Safari in Africa. No parents. No grandparents. Try as she might, she was finding it impossible to suppress the elated grin that lit up her face. Time to celebrate!

"Hey, Derek. Yeah, it's me, Shay. Listen... I'm just leaving school and the folks left for London this morning. I didn't see you at school today... guess you had more important things to do... but I was thinkin' that when the cats away, the mice should play! What do ya say? Party at my place?!" She was met with silence on the other end of the phone.

"Hello? Hello?! Are you there?" The call had been dropped. She scoffed loudly as she tossed her cell phone back into her bag. *"Piece of junk!* I'll call him later..."

Shayne Darby was never dissuaded from promoting her favorite cause. She referred to it fondly as, *The Charity of the Betterment of Shayne Darby!* Or... *CBSD*, for short. In her mind, success wasn't measured by the dollar figure in one's bank account, or by accumulating large quantities of diamonds or gold. At her age, true success could only be achieved by hosting the biggest party at the family estate... when her parents were unintelligent enough to leave her home alone for three weeks and a day! *Oh... all the possibilities!!*

Shayne was a pretty girl and she knew it. Her most striking features were her ice blue eyes and the freckles that dotted her nose and high cheekbones. With long, dark untamed hair, she was sassy and sexy and had the body that all boys talked about. As a matter of fact, her favorite phrase described her perfectly. *"I run wild and free and you can't catch me!"*

When she was young, her father used to tell her the story of her birth. He said that she was all bundled up when the stork delivered her, and the first thing that he saw was her tiny little nose and her rosy pink cheeks. The story goes that the heavens opened up. Sending down rain, the drops from above landed on the precious cargo, forever imprinting angel kisses on the wee bonnie lass.

The child within her liked to believe the tale to be true. Nobody else in the family had freckles so there had to be some truth to it.

Booming thunder brought Shayne back to the present. *Derek!* She had to go find him... or buy a new phone... or maybe just race home before the storm!

She dashed out of the schoolhouse doors, ran down the sidewalk, and picked up her pace with each thunderous boom and distant flash of light.

Glancing up at the menacing sky, she began to wonder if walking home was such a great idea. She should have bummed a ride. Too late! Thankfully, it wasn't a long trek home, and she'd be there before she knew it. At least that's what she kept telling herself.

When she was really little, she called storm clouds *hairy-scary clouds*. Today, she could see that the *hairy-scaries* were gathering and building over the mountain.

Shayne was a lot of things, but bravery failed her when storms were brewing. As a child, her mother's singing was the only thing that comforted her at times like these. Continuing down the sidewalk, she subconsciously began to hum the tune that her mother always sang to her in childhood. If Shayne were home, she'd be cowering bravely beneath a blanket on the couch... where lightning popped less frequently and thunder was only a muffled rumble.

The comforting song from days gone by came pouring out, as her eyes darted from the sidewalk... to the sky... then back to the sidewalk.

"Hairy-scary clouds can say... see us now, we cannot stay! We will race across the sky... hush little baby, please don't cry..."

When a wild crack of lightning hit the top of Mount Chloe, the frightened girl began running.

Loudly she sang, *"With our booming voice so near... we'll be leaving out from here! Hush little baby, please don't cry... hairy-scary clouds... GOODBYE!!"*

Her hair flew wildly behind her as she ran through the gate, up the driveway, over the brick walkway and into the safety of the house. It might have been her imagination, but the *hairy-scary clouds* seemed to be moving faster than normal. Either way, she was positive that that blanket was going to feel like a big warm hug when she finally made it to the soft leather couch.

THE STORM

The sky over Mount Chloe was taking on a life all its own as the storm began to intensify. Like a madman with a sword gripped firmly in his mighty hand, lightning slashed frantically across the darkness, while thunder reverberated between the surrounding mountains. The wind roared like a runaway freight train, threatening to derail, shaking the trees in its path.

Below, in the town of Chloe, word of impending danger from the approaching storm had gotten out, spreading like wildfire to the surrounding areas. Attempts were made to strap down potential flying objects, and shelter was sought by all that had breath within them.

Creatures of the forest, set in motion by natural instinct, ran seeking safety wherever it could be found as torrential rain descended from the monstrous clouds, pounding the earth and all that inhabited it.

Disasters like this didn't happen every day and this particular storm would soon go down in history as a once in a lifetime occurrence. Those who survived, were in agreement, that once... was one time too many.

The raging tempest swept across the land, eventually slowing down, only to hammer and destroy most everything in its path.

Hovering overhead for what seemed like hours, this storm that had so swiftly assailed them in the beginning, seemed in no hurry to depart. It raged on well into the night and fought desperately to hold back the morning light.

Water from above filled the rivers and creeks to overflowing, forcing the banks to release what had up until then, been held back safely. Floodwaters rushed wildly across the face of the land, sweeping away into the blackest of nights, those unable to reach higher ground. The howling wind would forever silence the screams of those less fortunate, as terror rained down upon them.

Like a weary marathon runner within sight of the finish line, the savage assault began stumbling and wobbling. Recognizing that the end was near, with a final gasp, it virtually collapsed on the other side of the mountain. In its wake, a wide swath of devastation stretched for miles and miles, leaving behind a scarred and battered landscape.

When peace finally settled upon the worn and the weary, hesitation caused many to pause and reflect on the previous hours of torment. Haunted by horrific sounds and horrendous visions, the living emerged cautiously from their shelters.

Never had a storm such as this come to visit a town such as theirs, and only time would be the healer as they gathered thoughts and counted blessings.

Prayers spiraled upward toward the heavens, giving hope and courage to many a grateful heart. Prayers, that poured forth from believers and unbelievers, alike.

DARKNESS

"In the beginning God created the heavens and the earth. The earth was without form and void; and darkness was on the face of the deep..." Genesis 1:1-2

Darkness had come to the small town of Chloe in the form of a man.

In the midst of the storm, he descended. Within the final bolt of deadly light, he was transported seemingly out of nowhere onto planet Earth. For that brief moment before his arrival, the slicing blade waved threateningly above all humanity, but it was sorrow's fateful bell that ultimately clanged, bringing evil to the mountaintop.

His feet landed on the precise location chosen for him, and he knew instantly that he was well suited for the work that lay ahead. A sinister smile formed on his chiseled face as he ran his smooth white hands through his dark wavy hair.

With steely fierceness blazing in his cold gray eyes, he stepped over the smoldering fire that had ignited near his feet. As smoke slowly billowed up behind him he proceeded to look for the simplest way down the mountainside.

Some of the terrain was easy going, but much of it was extremely rugged. Scrambling downward, he eventually neared the bottom, pausing to assess his condition. Noticing the mud and ash covering his boots, he bent over to wipe off as much of it as he could with a bandana he'd pulled from his pocket.

Satisfied with his appearance, he continued on until reaching the edge of the lake resting at the base of the mountain.

Skirting the shoreline, he located the dirt road leading to the paved road that would eventually take him to the highway. Fortunately, with the ground leveling out, he was then able to pick up his pace. He knew there was little time to spare if he was going to meet his contact and proceed as planned.

LIGHT

"... And the Spirit of God was hovering over the face of the waters. Then God said, "Let there be light"; and there was light."
Genesis 1:2-3

After the storm ceased, an unearthly stillness calmed the waters of Pale Moon Lake. Falling with arrowlike precision, the very last drop of rain fell from the sky, piercing the glasslike surface. The shimmering ripple that ensued, raced towards the pebbled shore. When it reached the beach, the water whispered, *'no more'* and the fluid dance ended, silently slipping away...

Time momentarily stood still, but nature's heartbeat cried out for balance, and the pendulum swung back to the present. The clouds parted and the sun's rays burst forth to shine brightly on the mirrored lake.

What came next was the ultimate response to previous darkness. *Illumination*, eclipsing all that was evil, boldly emerged from beneath the smooth surface of the water. *Light*, in the form of a second man... had arrived.

Simultaneously, the man of darkness, descending the mountain, stopped in his tracks as a shiver ran down his spine.

When the man of Light broke through the still surface, the birds of the heavens flew across the sky, welcoming the sun's warmth and his arrival. Rivulets of water streamed down the back of his neck and shoulders as he breathed in his first breath of clean, mountain air. Filling his lungs, he exhaled loudly, and praised God for all that was good.

His eyes opened slowly, revealing the vibrant color and richness of freshly tilled soil. They spoke of the endless depth of his soul, and unlike the steely gray eyes of the one brought forth by fire, this man emerging from the water had earth eyes shining brightly with the promise of new life.

With strong steady strokes, he began swimming for shore. As a mixture of joy and sorrow washed over him, he became more determined than ever to embrace them both. He was fully aware that he had arrived by divine appointment, and he was eager to accept his assignment. As was his adversary...

"And God saw the light, that it was good; and God divided the light from the darkness." Genesis 1:4

THE AFTERMATH

Jake leaned hard against the weathered door, pushing it open so that he and his grandfather could walk out onto what was left of their covered porch. The house looking out over Pale Moon Lake was battered, but still standing.

"Gramps... have you ever seen such a mess?"

Tears filled his eyes as Henry stared out over the property. Tree branches, boards from the barn and wood from the dock, lay scattered and tangled across the sweeping lawn. Shingles, broken shutters, twisted metal, shattered glass and debris littered almost every square inch of the property. There was obvious damage to the house, but the strong foundation and sturdy structure remained for the most part, miraculously intact.

Henry knew that the town of Chloe and surrounding area would be talking about this one for generations to come. At this point he could only imagine the far-reaching devastation. He was certain that there were those who didn't survive, but he also strongly believed that everyone would pitch in and carry the load. Neighbors would be helping neighbors and they'd all get through it, together.

When Henry was finally able to find his voice, he turned toward Jake and said, "Son, in all my years, and there have been many, I have never seen such a thing and never, have I experienced such an angry storm. The howling wind alone will be something I will never forget, but deep down inside I know there's a reason for everything. This storm didn't come here for nothing. It brought something. I can't explain it, but every fiber of my being says it will be revealed... one day."

"For now, I know that life is precious, and hope is the healing balm that chases away fear. When the sun's warmth returns to our broken land, healing will begin."

Jake believed that his grandfather spoke the truth. Something was different and it was more than just what his eyes were seeing. He sensed an ominous presence settling over the landscape before him. Something had shifted.

With mixed emotions, they stood side by side looking out over the lake. Although their mutual sense of foreboding was hard to shake, both knew that there was much work to be done and they needed to get started.

While time passed that day, the sun did make a brief appearance, and throughout the community, kindness was generously shared among the people. It was the widows and elderly that felt especially blessed. Hindered by age, life was not easy for those living alone, but there was a lot to be said for residing in a small town. In Chloe, when it came down to it, looking out for others was just the way it was done.

It had been a long day filled with hope and heartbreak, and sleep was longed for by all. After all, tomorrow was sure to bring new challenges and opportunities.

In the aftermath, as the sun dipped behind the mountains, and the full moon rose to reflect on Pale Moon Lake, the whispering wind carried simple truths...

Oil & vinegar could never mix and become one... and shadow and light would never be friends...

CHLOE

Nestled at the base of a jagged mountain range, Chloe was a friendly little town that knew no strangers. It had the reputation of being a safe place to live, and it was a great place to raise children. Chloe's inhabitants felt protected from the outside world and its unsavory influences. Kids could ride their bikes safely around town and hardly anyone locked their doors at night. The town itself looked like a page taken from a children's storybook. With fresh paint, flower boxes and a sense of order, it was the very definition of hometown America.

Between the mountains, there was only one way into the area and one way out, and the next town over was fifty miles away through a winding canyon. Just before entering Chloe, a beautifully lush valley was the *Welcome* mat that ushered visitors in.

Blue Sage Creek twisted and turned along the floor of the canyon, making the drive in and out of town a pleasant journey. Blue Sage was a sight to behold, especially in springtime when the snow on high melted sending the runoff racing down the mountain. Photographers flocked to the area to capture the magnificent display of nature in motion.

Winter, spring, summer and fall... the changing seasons were a shutterbug's absolute delight, and the economic boost they brought to the local shops, cafes and handful of inns, was greatly appreciated.

Seven miles beyond Chloe lay the prized jewel of the area. Resting in a pocket at the base of the mountain, Pale Moon Lake, was a dazzling gem. Legend had it that when the moon was full, if you were lucky enough to see your reflection on the surface of the lake at midnight, good things were destined to follow. There were many who boasted of catching a glimpse of themselves, but for the unlucky, it wasn't for lack of trying. The crystal-clear water was mesmerizing, and tranquil, and the banks of Pale Moon were quite popular when conditions were right.

Blue Sage Creek ran alongside the town of Chloe and traveled beyond it, eventually feeding into Pale Moon Lake. The highway continued on ten miles past the lake, but ended abruptly when the terrain said, *The End! (... and someone actually painted a sign shortly after the highway was finished, that said, THE END! It was nailed to a pine tree).*

A paved road exited the highway and wrapped three quarters of the way around the body of water. From there, the road turned to dirt and continued on. At the end of the dirt road was the *Mount Chloe Campground and Trailhead.* This valuable addition to the area enabled hikers and horseback riders to venture into the wilderness.

Camping was primitive. There were several tent sites, rugged parking spots for campers, and outhouses were the only option for those in need of restrooms. A small corral offered a temporary holding pen for horses and pack mules and a nearby natural artesian spring provided fresh water for drinking and washing up.

The campground was a great place to begin an adventure into high country. The trails extended for many a mile and the well-worn paths showed visible proof to the popularity of the journey. In the summer, hardy hikers and horseback enthusiasts kicked up their fair share of dust along the way.

Accompanied by creeks, waterfalls and various high mountain lakes, the weary travelers found refreshment along the way and in warm weather they enjoyed the beautiful wildflowers adorning the trail. It truly was an unforgettable journey leaving lasting impressions for those blessed enough to spend time in the high country.

Tourists and townspeople alike were of two different trains of thought when it came to sharing their experience in *God's Country*. Some wanted it to remain a hidden secret from the world... a place kept for them and them alone, while others wanted to advertise its existence to highlight all of the beauty nature provided.

In town, the business owners were always grateful for the economic boost generated by visitors and tourists. They believed that hospitality, clean water, abundant fishing, and many a clear and starry night, were gifts to be shared. And they were willing to open the doors wide to their little piece of paradise.

On the outskirts of town, spring's arrival was made official when the wildflowers bloomed in the meadow, turning the tender green grass into a blanket dotted with rich texture and vibrant color. It happened practically overnight.

A Chloe tradition came to be, way back in the early days. One spring morning, long ago, a man named Malachi Johnson witnessed the transformation in the meadow. He rode his horse into town and ran up the steps of the little clapboard church in the middle of town. He rang the church bell loud and clear which brought the townspeople to the steps below. He then proclaimed that spring had arrived and a celebration was in order!

After a lot of dancing, singing, whooping and hollering, it was decided that everyone would gather in the meadow for a feast... and Chloe's 1st Annual Springtime Flower Festival was born.

As years passed, the first Saturday in May became the designated day for the grand celebration. The community had always played a major role in its success. Some offered their time, some their manpower, and an account was also opened at the bank for monetary donations. All were of equal importance in making the tradition continue year after year.

At the festival you could expect to participate in a sack race, enjoy strawberry shortcake, and get conned into donating time in the dunking tank... all, while hearing the latest gossip from those in the know.

The Silent Auction was a popular *battle to be won*, as was the infamous Rubber Ducky Race. Participants in the race tossed a dollar in the bucket and chose a yellow rubber ducky from the inside of a bright red grocery cart. Each duck was assigned a number on its back. When the cap gun went off, everyone standing at the railing of the bridge, crossing over Blue Sage Creek, dropped their duck into the water below. The first bird to make it to the Chamber of Commerce Hut, 500 yards downstream, won the bucket full of cash, also known as the Pot-O-Gold. Enthusiasm was definitely the driving force that made the prize worth trying for.

The festival was known for its abundant humor and rowdy laughter. Each year, new stories were shared and memories were made and Chloe's Annual Springtime Flower Festival was sure to continue for many years to come.

DEREK

Derek Cyrus often wished he had never been born. As he sat at the lopsided kitchen table, silently struggling with dark persistent thoughts, he watched his mother scrub the day old, dried up, macaroni and cheese from the bottom of the pot. He couldn't help but think that her life could have been different had she not been stuck raising four sons on her own.

After his older brother, Dean, threw his last drug induced fit of rage, and proceeded to disappear, Derek was left bearing the weight of the strain that was placed on their mother. He witnessed her haggard face visibly aging before his eyes, and it was a heavy load to bear.

The way Derek saw it, Dean had willingly jumped feet first into the dark abyss as the cold cruel world grabbed him by the arm, jerking him out the door. Not knowing what to do, Derek froze in his tracks while he witnessed the traumatic event. When the last spark of life within his mother took flight, like a parakeet from an open cage, he felt paralyzed. Derek just stood there and watched. When the final slamming of the front door reduced Betty to a crumpled heap on the linoleum floor, there was no consoling her. She just laid there, sobbing uncontrollably, and Derek couldn't do a thing about it.

Two years had passed since Dean's cataclysmic departure and Betty's disabling heartache was still visible and palpable. Derek wished that he could erase the pain from her. Erase it with the flip of a knob on an Etch-N-Sketch, like he did when he was young, and still naïve to the hardships of the world. Those days were long gone, it seemed.

When you stare hard at something, really studying it, then look away, you can still see a shadowy image of the thing you were just staring at. But when you briefly glance at something, then turn from it, unless you wrap your mind tightly around that which was in front of you, the very memory of it fades quickly.

The difference between glancing and staring was huge, and the truth of the matter was, Betty would always see the shadowy image no matter how furiously Derek spun the knob trying to erase the past.

Derek's troubling thoughts were suddenly disrupted when his twin brothers charged full speed ahead, like two raging bulls, into the kitchen. Forced to abandon his private battlefield for theirs, Derek turned to face the unavoidable onslaught.

Dylan, the first beast to enter the arena, was wearing a stained T-shirt on inside out and backwards. Donald, flying in behind him in hot pursuit, grabbed on tightly to the back of his brother's shirt, ripping it as they flew by. With nostrils flaring, Donald shouted, "This is *my* shirt, not his! Make him give it back!"

Donald, no doubt, was a miniature version of Dean. His mannerisms and facial expressions were identical to their missing brother and Derek was always reminded of the loss when he looked at him. Dylan, on the other hand, looked more like their mother, which also translated as pain and heartache. Derek only hoped that his opinion of these two young brothers of his would change as they grew to be men.

Pushing himself away from the table, the folding chair Derek was sitting on scraped loudly as it slid across the peeling, linoleum floor.

Pointing back down the hallway, Derek hollered, "Out of here! Right now!! Get your sorry butts into your room and find something else to wear or you'll both be late for school!"

As they raced back down the hall, Derek's focus turned to his mother. Never lifting her eyes, she was steadily scrubbing the same pot, oblivious to the chaos around her.

Walking over to her side, he gently placed his hand on her shoulder. She kept on scrubbing. He dropped his hand to his side and slowly turned to walk to the door, pausing briefly to say, "Mom, I won't be home tonight for dinner." Betty just continued to clean the pot that no longer contained dried up macaroni and cheese.

Derek's temper tended to get the best of him. Hot one minute, cold the next. Turbulent thoughts twisted and turned after what appeared to be... *just another typical morning at the Cyrus house!* As he walked silently to school, he felt himself being pulled down a very dark and dangerous road.

"Snap out of it, Cyrus!" he mentally scolded himself. Usually, the thought of stopping off first at Shayne's house had a calming affect on him, but today was tougher than most. The picture of his mother's mental state left a heavy weight on his shoulders. It was too much to bear, in his mind.

"I gotta get out of here! I should just disappear like Dean... rotten degenerate! I don't have a car... I don't have any money...

how is that gonna work out?! How will mom take care of Dylan and Donald on her own? Oh yeah... rethink that! Not my problem! After all, they were her idea, not mine! None of us would be here if it were up to me! This is crap! But I could still leave home. Then mom could move off of the crappy couch and sleep in my bed... in that crappy house! Crappy life... crappy... CRAP!!"

If the old yellow Ford pickup truck driving past the scowling teen deep in thought had a conscience, it would surely have swerved, missing the pothole. But of course, it didn't. It hit the hole directly, going too fast in a 35, and muddy rainwater splattered all over Derek from head to toe.

"CRAAAAAAAAAAAP!!!"

Shayne was wrapping a towel around her wet head when the doorbell rang. *Derek!* She ran to the door, swinging it open wide.

"Didn't I tell you to always look to see who's at the door before opening it?!"

Shayne stared at her mud-covered friend, unwound the towel from her head and said, "Here, it looks like you need this more than I do."

A suppressed chuckle soon turned into uncontrollable laughter, but Derek wasn't thinking that the situation was all that funny.

Tripping over a stray shoe in the foyer, Shayne fell heavily against the wall.

"Serves you right..." grumbled Derek.

"Says YOU!" cried the girl, still laughing hysterically. She sat down on the bottom step of the stairs, rubbing her sore shoulder. A fit of laughter erupted once again from her as she imagined Derek looking like the local firehouse Dalmatian, Ambrose!

A volley of insults ensued, "Dalmatian!" "Hyena!!" "Dalmatian!!"

Derek headed to the downstairs shower while Shayne went back upstairs to retrieve clothes from her father's closet for her friend.

"No school today!" sang the happy teenager. She knew there was really no point in showing up late... and besides... with her parents out of town, a movie marathon at the house with Derek sounded like a better idea.

WILLOW

Willow was only fifteen years old when she gave birth to her first little *flower*, Daisy, and against her better judgement, she married Tad Wilson. When their baby was a mere four months old, Willow shared with Daisy's father, her belief that God wouldn't be giving them any more children. Tad was very happy to hear that.

One day, when the weary little mother was walking through the park with her bundle of joy riding safely in the stroller in front of her, Willow was convinced that she'd heard God speaking to her through the trees. She distinctly heard the leaves whispering... *only one... only one... only one...*

Six years later, after a home pregnancy test confirmed that she didn't have the flu and that Daisy was going to have a sibling, Tad didn't hold back his feelings on the matter.

"ONLY ONE, Willow?! You meant... ONLY ONE MORE!! I swear, woman, you NEVER listen!! You should have been on birth control, or better yet, Doc Jones should have spayed you long ago like he did *Sparkles*... that worthless old hound dog of yours!"

Willow had heard enough to know that she, Daisy and her unborn child were never going to have to hear another hurtful word from Tad Wilson! At that very moment, her plan of escape began forming in her mind.

One dark night, while her verbally abusive husband was sleeping off the effects of an evening spent at the local pub, Willow made her move. In her eighth month of pregnancy, she quietly packed up Daisy, her *Beatles* album collection and everything else deemed useful, and her old yellow Ford pickup truck carried them off into the night.

Willow left no note behind and she never looked back. 1,823 miles later... when "Buttercup" sputtered and broke down just outside of Chloe, Willow smiled at Daisy, rubbed her swollen belly, and professed to her girls, "Looks like we've found our new home!"

Shortly thereafter, Sweet Pea was delivered safely into the arms of her loving mother. And thanks be to Grandma Ida and Grandpa Ezra James, *may they rest in peace.* The financial inheritance they'd left to Willow, allowed her to purchase a cozy little cottage on ten acres of land. They had escaped a life of anger and uncertainty and Willow was grateful. She knew that God had led them to Chloe for a reason and in time they would realize all of the blessings He had in store for the three of them.

Sadness, oftentimes came to visit in waves, when memories of her grandparent's tragic death were brought to mind. A house fire of all things. Willow believed that the fire could have been prevented, and she was doubly saddened by the fact that her grandparents would never experience the joy that her tiny flowers had to give. Along with the grief, sweet memories also came to mind. Her grandparents raised her from birth in a home filled with lots of love and humor and Willow was very determined that her girls would experience the same.

Shortly after the devastating loss of the only parents Willow would ever know, an attorney showed up on her doorstep with a briefcase containing a will that left all of their belongings and money to Willow. It was a lot to digest as she had no idea that her grandparents had attained such wealth. They had all lived such a simple life, just the three of them.

In those early days without them, after realizing that she was financially secure, something within her told her to keep this family secret just that, a secret. And so, she did. Tad Wilson never knew that his wife was a wealthy woman, and in hindsight that was a total blessing. Willow knew that Tad would have gambled and drank away every dime of it, if it had fallen into his hands.

The young mother immediately transferred her sizeable nest egg into the local bank, after arriving in Chloe. She also made sure that the bank she'd left behind would not reveal her whereabouts to Tad. Small towns tend to gossip, and she did not want her past colliding with the future that she'd envisioned for her and the girls.

When choosing the land, Willow looked for a sturdy home, a good water source, and rich soil. She had long dreamed of tending a garden filled with flowers, and growing healthy plants would provide the necessary blossoms and blooms to bless her community with colorful, fragrant bouquets.

It was a reoccurring nightmare that initially planted the seed for Willow to bring joy and happiness to the world… via bundles of flowers. She pushed against the repetitive nightmare, and eventually a sweet dream emerged. Daisy was just three years old when it all began…

The Garden of Eden was a place of unexplainable beauty. Everything appeared more vibrant, more lush, more abundant, and larger than life. Lungs breathed in pure oxygen, and the air was alive with birdsong.

Eve walked amongst the tranquil foliage with the forbidden fruit held tightly in the palm of her hand. Transfixed by its beauty and sheen, she was unable to take her eyes off of it.

Suddenly, a hissing noise in the undergrowth caused her to abruptly shift her gaze away from the fruit. The birds stopped singing, and all became quiet and still.

Willow stepped from behind a nearby tree and snapped her fingers, breaking the trance. Eve turned and locked eyes with her, and a strange and powerful look washed over Eve's face.

"Take a look around you, Eve... take a really good look! Put it back! Trust me... I know what I'm talking about..."

Continuing to stare at Willow, Eve just tightened her grip on the piece of fruit in her hand. Her eyes then shifted, once again, and were held captive by its beauty.

Suddenly, the ground began to shake violently and a large limb from above fell, hitting Willow on the top of her head...

Willow awakened immediately. With tears glistening in her eyes, she couldn't help but to think how differently things could have been for all of them, if only Eve had made a better choice. One thing was for sure, Willow was determined to choose wisely from there on out, when it came to her and her girls' future.

Her property was nestled in the valley with a stunning view of the mountains. The growing season was a challenge as it tended to be shorter in the slightly higher elevation, but she eventually built a good-sized greenhouse to help lengthen the season. All things considered, Willow was extremely pleased at how well she and the girls were adapting to their new life. Her business, *Blossoms & Blooms,* was proving to be all that she had hoped it would be, and she was blessed with two healthy daughters. Life was good.

Willow and Daisy designed and painted the business logo on both sides of her old yellow Ford, *Buttercup,* and Sweet Pea added her tiny handprints for good luck.

That first spring, Willow hired carpenter Henry Davis to build a quaint barn to sell the flowers out of, and a greenhouse to grow them in. The barn, complete with an office, a small kitchenette and a restroom, became an extension of their living quarters on many a day.

Willow and Daisy painted an *Open* and *Closed* sign for the barn. On one side of the old wooden shingle there were brightly painted flowers waving in the breeze beneath the bright sunshine. On the opposite side, there were tightly closed blossoms beneath the light of the full moon.

As years passed, and the girls grew older, Daisy looked more and more like her beautiful mother. With their golden skin, long blonde hair and bright, sky blue eyes, there was no denying that they belonged to one another. Sweet Pea was cast from the same mold as her mother and sister, although her coloring was different. Her skin was golden brown, as was her hair, and her eyes were the palest shade of green. Willow marveled at the variation of her two favorite blossoms.

Willow counted her blessings, daily, and the day came when she knew it was time to sever her ties from the past. She contacted the same lawyer who handled her grandparents will, and asked him to write up divorce papers to be served on Tad Wilson. It was long overdue.

The divorce was handled quickly and without incident as Tad was more than willing to sign away his wife and children. Although he could have asked to be a part of Daisy and Sweet Pea's lives, he never did. That fact alone was more than enough to convince Willow that they were all better off without him!

A pleasant change was coming to the Wilson's. One, that would take them all by surprise. As the sisters thrived in the fresh mountain air and Willow's dream flourished, the unimaginable occurred. Willow made room in her heart for *one more...*

His name was Jack Sanders. Jack was the proud owner and sole proprietor of *Jack Sander's Gently Used Cars,* and Jack was the polar opposite of Tad Wilson.

Many years earlier, Jack was engaged to Darcy Woods. She was his first true love and he was happy to call her his fiance`e, if only for a brief period of time. As it turned out, it was not destined to end well.

Darcy painfully and publicly humiliated Jack in front of the entire town at the Annual Flower Festival. She showed up at the celebration, drunk, wearing a skimpy outfit on her curvy figure and Darren Talmander on her arm.

At the height of the festival, she noisily grabbed the microphone from the festivities director and proceeded to tell the world and all of Chloe that "Jack Sanders would never be anything but an overweight car salesman AND she and Darren were heading to *New York City*!"

She yanked the engagement ring Jack had given her off of her finger and tossed it into the nearby dunking tank. She then spun on her high heels, snapping one off, and hobbled out of the park on Darren's arm... never to be seen or heard from again!

When the dust finally settled that day, and the sun began to set, Clancy Arnold dove to the bottom of the tank to retrieve Jack's ring. Jack quietly thanked Clancy, and with downcast eyes and drooping shoulders, he walked home alone.

Two years later, Jack had healed enough to take the engagement ring to the pawn shop so he could donate the money to the local church where he and Darcy would have been married. A few years after that, a rainbow finally arrived when the seemingly unending stretch of rain, ceased.

Jack just happened to be passing through the produce section on his way to the bakery in Bailey's Grocery Store, when he caught his first close up glimpse at the woman who grew flowers in the valley.

Willow was happily chatting with Mr. Bailey when Jack tripped over a display of pumpkins, sending them rolling in every direction. He simply could not take his eyes off of her as he lost his balance and fell flat on his back on the floor. The next thing he knew, Mr. Bailey and Willow were standing over him asking him if he was okay. He was pretty sure that he was not okay, because the woman standing over him had to be an *angel*!

Jack's life changed dramatically for the better from that day forward. He joined the gym, lost 35 pounds, and secretly vowed to marry his angel before the year was up.

Several months later, he worked up the courage to ask Willow out to dinner and she accepted the invitation. At the restaurant, they discovered that they had a lot in common, and they easily enjoyed each other's company. From that point forward, they began dating regularly.

It didn't take Jack long to take his grandmother's brilliant white diamond to the jewelers to have a ring made. This one would be a special one, deserving of his grandmother's prized gemstone. It was set into the center of a beautiful flower made from gold, and Jack tucked the ring away for safe keeping.

Two months later, when the moon was full, Jack kneeled down on one knee, professed his love and asked Willow to be his wife. On the banks of Pale Moon Lake, his angel said, "Yes! Oh, yes!!"

After the Darcy Woods debacle, the townspeople believed Jack would never marry. Happy were they, when they heard that a wedding would soon take place.

On a beautiful summer day, in the little white church in Chloe, Jack and Willow, surrounded by friends, family and abundant flowers, exchanged their vows. A joyous celebration followed as the church bells rang loud and clear.

Jack, Willow, Daisy and Sweet Pea were meant to be a family. Several months later, Willow confirmed it when she whispered in her handsome husband's ear, "... we are the happily-ever- afters, Jack. I know this because I heard it on the breeze today..."

DAISY

Daisy whistled and waved at her mother and sister as she stepped off of the school bus. Both of them looked up at the same time and smiled, waving back. Just seeing them tending the flowers in the garden reminded Daisy of how lucky she was to have them in her life. Her mother brought sunshine, even on the dreariest of days, and Sweet Pea was blessed with the gift of humor. Laughter was good medicine and her little sister had plenty of that to share with all of them.

As far as Daisy was concerned, Jack was also a blessing worth counting. He was kind and loving towards their mother and he was shaping up to be a pretty good stepfather. He was a bit hesitant in the beginning, when it came to knowing what to do with three females in the house, but he proved to be a fast learner. Jack discovered quickly that girls were emotional at times, and tinkering on small projects in the barn was a great idea, when necessary.

Daisy, strong willed and sometimes easily agitated, often thought that it must have come from her biological father's side. She tried hard to keep her attitude in check and was mostly successful in doing so, but Wallace Kramer, her friend and nemesis, could frustrate her faster than anyone else on the planet. That boy, that boy!

Daisy headed from the bus to the house and as she neared the gate, she tipped her head up towards the sun and whispered, *"Home sweet home..."*

School was fairly easy for Daisy and she thrived on education and learning, but she was beyond thrilled that graduation was on the horizon. As much as she loved her mother, sister and Jack, she was eager to move onto college when the summer was over. Daisy would be sad to leave Sweet Pea behind. Her sister was easy to be around, as far as sisters went, and she never could figure out why school had become such a different experience for Sweet Pea. Her little sister had to be brought home to be home schooled in the fifth grade.

Sweet Pea was that puzzle piece that just didn't fit somehow, when it came to education. She saw things in a different way than her peers and her teacher, and Mrs. Honeywell thought she was a distraction in the classroom. She told Willow that... *"her thinking did not align with the other children... and detention for a week might straighten her out."* Willow disagreed.

Sweet Pea was immediately removed from Chloe Elementary and her mother proceeded to turn their dining room at home into a classroom for her daughter. In the months that followed, Willow's youngest flower literally blossomed before her eyes. What worked for one child, did not always work for the next.

Daisy needed interaction with her schoolmates and she embraced life at Chloe High. She felt that she was blessed with a brilliant mind and common sense, two things that would hopefully carry her far in life. Wallace, on the other hand, had a brilliant mind and zero common sense. He was a challenge to her.

Willow's eldest flower was ready to sprout wings and fly. She was looking forward to stepping out of the box, to test the waters, and the senior class camping trip was just the place to do it. One glorious week away from her everyday existence and who knew what might transpire on the mountaintop? She did know that Wallace was feeling like a heavy anchor pulling her down. He wanted to keep her in the box she was so eager to jump out of... therefore, she would have to come up with a plan for him.

Think... think... think...

Plan A: *Maybe... Wallace could fall in love with Minnie... I mean Claire Mathews. Love could certainly distract him! Though plain, Claire seemed nice... in a very quiet way... but she would definitely have to bust out of that shell of hers. Might not be possible. Better try Plan B!*

Plan B: *Maybe... Wallace could be encouraged to catch a miserable cold. He could either stay at home altogether and miss the trip... or spend his time bundled up in his assigned cabin with a box of tissue and a humidifier. Wow. Not very nice, Dais! Think, think, think...*

Plan C: *Pay a fellow student to keep him chasing after rare butterflies and spiders in the woods. Convince him that if he keeps looking, he will surely find the missing link. Brilliant! Plan C it is!*

THE MEADOW

A few months after the storm of all storms had passed, spring awoke from its slumbering nap, shaking its fist at winter. With the sun's warm rays shining down from above, bright yellow, pink and blue flowers began popping their sleepy heads up from the sunkissed ground... and Walden... Chloe's favorite mailman... was there to see it!

He could not wait to be the first one to ring the church bell! He'd wanted to do the honors ever since he'd moved to Chloe ten years earlier, but each spring, there was always someone else in the meadow at the right time... beating him to it. Not this year! This was Walden's lucky year!

Walden and his mail truck came careening into town, taking the final turn on two wheels, barely missing Cromwell, the mayor's favorite dog. With horn honking and lights flashing, his tires squealed as he came to a screeching halt in front of Blue Sage Community Church.

Walden jumped out of the truck and quickly ran up the steps of the church. On his way up the stairs, he hollered over his shoulder, "Sorry, Cromwell!"

Hearing all of the commotion out front, Pastor Tom met Walden at the door. "Walden, for heaven's sake, man, what in the world has gotten into you?"

"Gotta ring the church bell, Pastor Tom. Spring is here! Gotta shout it from the rooftop! The wildflowers found their way to the meadow, despite that ghastly storm we had. Come on Pastor, we gotta ring it loud and proud! Spring is here!!"

Walden almost knocked the good man down on his way to the inner staircase. Pastor Tom just smiled, shook his head, and followed Walden up the stairs. He knew that the excited mailman was probably thinking of Frieda Gayle's strawberry shortcake... and what the future held. He was fairly sure that it was going to taste especially delicious this year at the Flower Festival, what with Walden being the ringer of the bell.

For years, it was common knowledge about town that Walden had been the biggest supporter of Frieda's shortcake sales. In addition, he had an ulterior motive. Each time he bought the prized dessert from her, he asked for her hand in marriage. Frieda's reply was always the same, "Not until you ring the church bell when spring arrives. It will be a sign from God that you are the man for me... but not until then!" Pastor Tom knew that this year would be a memorable one.

Taking a pair of ear plugs from his pocket, he pressed them firmly into his ears. The church bell was clanging loudly, well before the pastor ever reached the top step.

All over town, doors flew open and people of all shapes and sizes filled the sidewalks and flooded the streets. As the bell tolled, shopkeepers danced with customers and city workers kicked up their heels in wild abandon. *Tradition!*

Dogs howled loudly when music was cranked up from a nearby delivery truck, and children chased each other around town in a game of tag. Excitement rippled in contagious fashion, as happiness radiated from the faces of the merrymakers. This was just what the doctor ordered after the winter they'd all recently survived.

When the sound of the church bell reached the courthouse, the doors swung wide and Daniel Kramer obediently dragged the P.A. system down the street behind Mayor MacFarland. The annual speech given on this occasion by Fink MacFarland was expected to occur in the center of town. When the mayor and Daniel arrived there, Daniel plugged the system into the electrical outlet in front of Frieda Gayle's Bakery.

They waited until the bell in the steeple stopped ringing. Shortly thereafter, the dancing subsided and everyone crowded around the mayor to hear what he had to say.

Mayor MacFarland grabbed the mic from Daniel and stepped up onto the overturned crate that Fred Mathews had provided from his hardware store.

"Bless my soul... what a beeeeee-uuu-ti-ful-daaaaay!!" proclaimed the overweight, red faced mayor. "First, I'd like to thank Danny Boy, for setting up this sound system!" "Danny Boy... remind me to give you a raise when we get back to the courthouse!"

The townspeople clapped their hands and chuckled at Mayor Fink MacFarland's announcement. Daniel, on the other hand, attempted a smile as he grumbled under his breath... *"Sure thing, Fink! That'll happen when pigs fly..."*

"What was that, Danny Boy?"

Daniel, the mayor's bespeckled accountant, pushed his glasses back up the bridge of his nose, turned towards the mayor and said, "Uh... I said you bet, sir! Will do!"

Clearing his throat, Mayor MacFarland continued his speech.

"HEAR YE... hear YEEEEEEE... Let me just say that this is my FAVORITE season OF the YEARRR!!"

Those near enough to be assaulted by the loud sound coming from the P.A.'s speaker, quickly covered their ears with their hands.

Fink paused to fiddle with the volume on the screeching speaker, then whispered to his accountant, "Danny Boy, make a note! We need to buy a new P.A. system."

"WALDEN PHILLIPS says the MEADOW is bloooooomin' and Harley TANNER will BE settin' UP HIS CAMEEEERA ONCE again near Tucker's BEND... take picTURES... A FEE!"

Daniel Kramer tried diligently to correct the technical difficulties. *Where was Wallace when he needed him?*

The mayor continued, "Any AND ALL... who want a picture taken IN THE FLOWERS... can meet Harley THERE... Lunch!"

The confused onlookers wondered if he'd said, *before... or was it... after lunch?*

"WALDEN will get a $50.00 gift CERTIFICATE to Mathews HardWARE store... where I hope he'll USE IT ON WHITE paint for THAT picket FENCE of his. It's looking PRETTY SHABBBBBBY! Or maybe SOME BAIT... for fishing THIS WEEKEND!!!! Or some WEEEEED Killer for HIS YARD!! Maybe some shells for duck HUNTING, after we go fishin'... or... OH HECK... it's yours TO spend WALDEN! DO what you like...CONGRATULATIONS!"

"OK... I'll shut UP NOW! Esther is giving ME THE looooook! Yeah... you KNOW the look, ESTHER. Yep! THAT ONE! God LOVE ya Esther! Anyhow... let's just ROLL up OUR SLEEVES and PUT in the work, FOLKS, to make the SPRIIIIING Festival THE best one YET! I can't HELP but laugh when I THINK OF last year's FEST..." Screeeeeeech.... Click!

The P.A. system died and Daniel and Esther breathed a simultaneous sigh of relief. Mayor MacFarland never skipped a beat as he continued laughing and talking into the microphone. Eventually, he did get the message that his speech was over, when Daniel pulled the plug on the sound system, and took the mic from his hand.

The lingering crowd shared ideas for the upcoming festival and Walden Phillips received congratulations along with well wishes. Standing shyly nearby, Frieda Gayle straightened her flour covered apron and tried to contain her smile. Walden winked at her right before she turned to go back inside her bakery.

Soon, everyone would disperse, and the sun would dip down behind the mountain. The moon would rise up in the nights sky, and the little town of Chloe would be lulled to sleep by the singing sound of night birds and crickets.

Walden doubted that he'd be able to sleep that night. After all, he had a proposal to plan. This time it would have to be special, and a bouquet from *Blossoms & Blooms* would be a great place to start in the morning...

GOING WITH THE FLOW

Esther Brumble, Mayor Fink's beloved secretary, was the self-appointed committee leader for Chloe's Annual Springtime Flower Festival. Each year, after the wildflowers made their appearance, a meeting was held at Charlie's Coffee Cup & Café, and this year would be no different.

When the committee gathered in the café the following morning, the coffee flowed liberally and breakfast was served. The food was as terrific as ever, and Charlie's coffee was predictably thicker than most. Although it didn't appeal to all coffee drinkers, the locals who frequented *The Cup*, were used to it. Of course, cream and sugar helped to make it more palatable, and both were definitely in high demand at Charlie's place. Twenty years in the food industry and he only made the mistake one time, of running out of both cream and sugar. After that, he swore he'd never do that again! It was bad for business.

The diners were happily chatting and eating, but before everyone could finish their meal, Esther stood up and pounded her miniature gavel on the cafe's breakfast counter.

"MAY I HAVE YOUR ATTENTION PLEASE?! THIS MEETING WILL NOW COME TO ORDER!!"

Esther stepped behind the counter where she could better face the crowd.

"Last year's festival was a tremendous success and I have printed out copies of the same game plan for this year."

Frieda Gayle immediately raised her hand, "I have a question, Esther. Where will I be setting up my Strawberry Shortcake stand? Every year I'm right next to the Dunking Tank, and my customers are tired of getting wet while standing in line. I'd rather be closer to the Silent Auction, where it's calmer... but upwind from the Barbeque Grill. I don't want to have my clothes and hair smelling like smoke."

"Now Frieda, I will do my best to place everyone accordingly, but I will make no promises. I'll be posting the booth assignments on the courthouse bulletin board as soon as it's finalized. Hopefully, by early next week. We have to give folks time to submit their requests for a space. Now... if I may be allowed to continue..."

"Esther, I have a question too!" Fred Mathews stood up when he spoke, knocking over his coffee cup. A young waitress on her first day at the café, hustled over with a wet rag to clean up the mess.

"I am soooo sorry!" professed Fred.

After the coffee was wiped up and Fred's cup refilled, he continued with his question.

"I'd really like to have a raffle at my booth this year and our cat had kittens several weeks ago. I figured I could raffle off a carpeted cat condo... and give the kittens away for free... along with a bag of kitten food and a free flea collar, of course. So, my question is, do you mind if we bring Skittle's and her babies to the festival this year?"

"Fred, bring them if you must, but don't expect me to take one home with me. I'm highly allergic!" she replied.

Four more people raised their hands as Walden proceeded to say, "Esther, I have a question too!"

"THAT'S IT! No more questions!! I said... I have copies of the game plan from last year and we're sticking to it!" Esther passed the papers around as quickly as she could.

"You will all just have to go with the flow! And if you can't, well then, just go with God, because time's up and I need to get back to the office! THIS MEETING IS ADJOURNED!!"

With that, Esther pounded her gavel on the counter one last time and tossed it into her red handbag. Spinning on her heel she headed for the door and was gone.

Frieda turned to Walden and Fred and said, "Well... I guess she told us."

Across town, the high school gymnasium was alive with chattering teenagers and squeaking tennis shoes, as Chloe's senior class was being assembled to discuss the upcoming class camping trip. As the students scrambled up the wooden bleachers to claim their spot, Mr. Sherman and Miss Trent asked for their attention.

"Ok everybody, listen up! This won't take long if everyone quiets down and cooperates!"

Dax Sherman, the senior boy's class advisor, turned to Naomi Trent, the senior girl's advisor, and held up a stack of handouts.

"If you wouldn't mind, Miss Trent."

Smiling warmly, she happily received the stack of papers from her handsome colleague, and with agility and grace, she ascended the right side of the bleachers, handing multiple copies to the students sitting at the end of each seat.

"Thank you, Miss Trent. Now, would the person on the end please take one and pass the rest on down the line. If you run out, we have more!"

Miss Trent made it safely back down to the polished wooden floor and returned to Mr. Sherman's side.

"Ok... senior class trip! Very important! In your handout you will find a list of necessary items that you will not want to leave home without! For starters... a pillow! A sleeping bag! Plenty of insect repellant AND MOST IMPORTANTLY... SUNSCREEN! A swimsuit, towels, a toothbrush, toothpaste, soap, shampoo, notebook, etc. It's all there. Please, please, please take the time to go over it carefully and it'll be helpful if you check off each item from the list as you pack them! There will be no trips down off the mountain to retrieve forgotten things! Cellphones, however, must intentionally be left behind because they are not welcome!" "Ok, Naomi... I mean Miss Trent... I'll let you take it from here."

"Thank you, Mr. Sherman." "Alright, everybody, may I have your attention?! I know those bleachers are not all that comfortable and I will try to make this brief! Let me begin by saying that we have so enjoyed our previous trips to Soaring Eagle Lodge with the various seniors over the past several years, and we truly hope that this year will be no exception. Spending a week surrounded by the best that nature has to offer can be life altering. You may wonder, *how so*, when we already live in one of the most beautiful locations on Earth, but to get high up amongst the clouds... well, truly, it is an experience that you will never forget!"

"I plan on getting high amongst the clouds!" shouted someone from the bleachers.

Mr. Sherman took a step forward, "Excuse me... who said that?! Was that you, Derek? Would you like to have the floor?

The Rain Mender

Do you have something more important to say than Miss Trent... something that you'd like to share with your fellow classmates?!"

"I didn't say anything, Mr. Sherman. It wasn't me!"

"Ok, listen up! I WILL be talking to you, Derek, after the assembly, but while we're on the subject... pardon me for interrupting you, Miss Trent... it is important that you all realize that there will be NO DRUGS OR ALCOHOL tolerated on this class trip! I repeat... NO DRUGS OR ALCOHOL.... AT ANY TIME! If I have to, I will personally escort any and all offenders back to their respective parents quicker than you can say, 'WASN'T ME!' Now, please continue, Miss Trent."

"Thank you for addressing that issue, Mr. Sherman." "Now, I would like to add that we will be staying in assigned cabins. The lodge is run by Mr. Thaddeus Barron. He is the owner and operator and is a wonderful man. He takes great pride in Soaring Eagle Lodge and I encourage you all to be respectful. If he asks you to carry firewood into the lodge, please lend a hand. You will find that he is a most gracious host and he has a delightful sense of humor. Let's all just go with the flow... follow the rules... and make our principal and parents proud! Thank you."

Naomi took a step back while Dax stepped forward once again.

"The bus leaves Monday morning after the Springtime Flower Festival... 6:00 a.m. sharp! BE ON TIME! We won't wait on late stragglers! You are dismissed... except for you, young man!" Mr. Sherman pointed his finger at Derek Cyrus.

Derek remained seated at the top of the bleachers and Mr. Sherman waited for the students to return to class before addressing the issue with him.

Climbing up the bleachers, he sat down next to him.

"Derek, I want to encourage you to cut the crap... and to be on your best behavior on this trip. I know things aren't always easy at home, but you and I are not all that different from one another. I've been in your shoes. Things can improve, but it's up to you to make the change. I want you to know that I understand, and I'm here for you. I'd also like to help you get your gear together. I have an extra sleeping bag as well as some supplies and I know that I won't be able to use all of them myself. I'm going to leave a box by your backdoor on Saturday. Just look through it and see if you can use any of it. If not, pass it on to someone else. More importantly, I'm hoping you'll keep those feet of yours on the ground and that head of yours out of the clouds. There's a lot more to life than getting high… and I'm sure that one day you'll realize it. Anyhow, do me a favor and let's have a good trip! Ok?"

Derek kept his eyes on his feet and just nodded his head slowly.

MICHAEL

The baby blue and white Volkswagen van purred like a well-fed mountain lion cub as it hummed down the highway. Older vans like these were rarely found in mint condition and he knew that he had been blessed beyond measure. Reflecting back on his good fortune, Mabel Carmichael was someone he would never forget. And repaying her a visit one day, to thank her again for her kindness and generosity, was something he genuinely looked forward to.

The story of her husband William's, sudden and tragic passing just days after purchasing the van, touched Michael's heart. He couldn't imagine the devastation Mabel must have felt when the deputy showed up on her doorstep. Giving her the tragic news that a plane crash had crushed the future dreams held by the happily married young couple, was difficult to fathom.

When the Carmichael's were newly married, they shared a similar dream of touring as many National State Parks as possible. Visiting all 50 states was a goal they had set together.

When William's wealthy uncle passed away, having no children of his own, he left the majority of his prosperity to his only nephew. Thanks to his uncle's generosity, it looked like the newlyweds dream of travel was bound to come true, sooner than anticipated. If not for a commercial jet going down in a snow storm on that fateful day, the sky was the limit for the two young people, but it was extremely sad to have this tragic event follow such a tremendous blessing.

Soon after William was laid to rest, Mabel closed the garage door on their van and their mutual dream, and there it remained, for all those years... until today.

As Michael stood waiting in line at the grocery store, the elderly woman in front of him slowly turned around, looking him straight in the eyes.

"Young man, there's something at my house that belongs to you." She picked up her small bag of groceries and headed for the front door of the store.

After paying for the deli sandwich, candy bar and soda, he too went out through the door of the market, and found her waiting for him. He gently lifted the grocery bag from her arms, and offered to carry it for her. As it was, her home was just a short walk down the sidewalk.

The white cottage with the light blue shutters seemed fitting for a grandmother. Behind the white picket fence, a beautiful flower garden adorned the front yard, and a brick path led the way to the wooden front door.

She opened the door, inviting him in. After placing her groceries on the kitchen table, he followed her into what appeared to be a small library with a fireplace. Reaching up, she retrieved a set of keys that were hanging on a hook at the end of one of the bookcases.

"Please, follow me if you will," she said softly.

Together, they went out the backdoor and walked to an overgrown, detached garage. It was obvious that without attention, ivy had been growing up and over it for many years.

"My Parkinson's is acting up, so if you wouldn't mind opening the garage door, I would be very appreciative."

She handed the young man the keys. He obliged her and the ancient door creaked loudly as dust showered down upon him from above.

Inside the garage, the van was concealed beneath what appeared to be a custom cover. She asked him to remove it and when he did, he couldn't believe what he saw. The powder blue & white Volkswagen van looked as though time had stood still. It was in pristine condition, inside and out.

"It was brand new when we bought it. William was so proud of it. He could hardly wait to get it out on the open road. He was off on a last-minute business trip, and after that, we had plans to hit the road and travel. It was not meant to be..."

Her eyes welled up with tears as she turned to him, pointing to the set of keys that she'd carried in her hand from the library.

"There are only 38 miles on the odometer. I hope and pray that you will drive it in good health. I've kept it safely in this garage all of these years. A dear friend, who happens to be a mechanic, has looked in on it periodically for me... changing the oil, the fluids, keeping it clean and running... and today, a voice within me said, *'Mabel, turn around and give the van to Michael.'* Your name is Michael, yes?"

"Yes ma'am... my name is Michael Rain."

"Well, Michael Rain, those keys are yours, and may your travels be blessed abundantly. In addition to keys to the van, you'll also notice another key. William built a small log cabin back in the early days on Pale Moon Lake, just outside of a little town named Chloe. We spent weekends there, our first summer together. It's a magical lake near a friendly community and if you talk to the manager at the campground on the lake, he can direct you to the Carmichael cabin. Just tell him that Mabel sent you and show him the key... as it's rather unique. The cabin is yours for as long as you need it."

Mabel gently reached for Michael's hands. Covering his strong tanned hands with her pale, feeble ones, her face lit up with an endearing smile that reached her eyes.

"Go with God, Michael."

When their eyes met, he gently replied, "Always."

With a map of the area on the passenger's seat and a full load of supplies in the back, Michael left the city and headed back to Pale Moon Lake. The drive through the canyon along the creek was a pleasant one and he rolled down the windows to enjoy the fresh, spring air. He looked forward to locating the Carmichael cabin, settling in, and beginning his work.

With the Springtime Flower Festival just around the corner, he'd have plenty to keep his hands busy and his mind occupied. Michael was certain that in the nearby woods he would be able to find some small pine burls to make displays for his handiwork. The jewelry he created was very unique, truly like no other, and he genuinely enjoyed the journey of turning something primitive in appearance, into something of great beauty.

Soon, he would be able to share his gift with those around him. His labor of love was intended to bless beyond measure, and he was grateful to God for all that had been given to him, but more importantly, he felt humbled, when his gift reached out and blessed others...

When Michael arrived at the campground on Pale Moon Lake, he was welcomed by Forest Service Ranger, Bud Parker. Ranger Bud was a jovial man with a strong handshake and an infectious smile. Michael, an excellent judge of character, could tell instantly that he was trustworthy, and the obvious choice for managing the camping area and the handful of privately owned cabins along the lakeshore.

After introducing himself, Ranger Bud invited Michael inside his comfortable, well organized office. The walls were adorned with topographical maps, photographs of the area's wildlife, while a sturdy wooden desk, centrally located, anchored the room. There was a small leather couch resting along the opposing wall, facing the desk.

"Have a seat young man. Can I offer you a cup of coffee or a cold soda?"

"No... thank you. I don't want to interrupt your day. I was just hoping that you could direct me to the Carmichael cabin. Miss Mabel told me to stop in here and show you the key to the cabin. She's been kind enough to offer it to me while I'm here for the Flower Festival."

"Heavens, yes! I'd be happy to! If you don't mind, I can jump in my jeep and you can follow me. There are a few twists and turns in the road and it's easier if I just show you the way."

"That would be great, if it's no trouble?"

"No trouble at all! Anyhow, I like to check on the cabins periodically, and now is as good a time as any. Just follow me!"

The Ranger grabbed the keys to his jeep from a hook on the wall by the door, he put a sign in the window, stating that he would be back shortly, and the two men then stepped out of the office into the fresh mountain air.

From the campground's office, the Carmichael cabin was approximately a ten-minute drive down a dirt road. When they rounded the last bend and came out into a small clearing, Michael was greeted by a gorgeous view of the lake. Turning his gaze towards the log cabin, in a word, it was simply, charming!

Michael parked the van next to Ranger Bud's jeep, and followed him up the steps onto a spacious deck that was facing the lake.

"Wow! This is beautiful!" exclaimed Michael.

"Yes, it is! Mr. Carmichael knew what he was doing building his cabin in this location. This one has probably the best view out of all of those built here. He was a good man, and his missus has a heart of gold! Good folks." Shaking Michael's hand, he continued to say, "... well, I best be getting back to the office, in case visitors need to check in or out. If you have any questions, just come on back and I'll try to answer them. Enjoy your stay, Michael!"

"Thank you, sir. I'm sure I will."

The key to the cabin was fairly slim, even though it appeared to be made from cast iron. The wooden door was heavy, had black hinges and a decorative lock. It had a small window towards the top, which allowed the occupants to see who, if anyone, came knocking.

After stepping inside, Michael couldn't help but smile. The cabin was warm and cozy, and furnished as one would imagine it should be. Handmade furniture built from local timber graced the spacious living area. There were blue and white checked curtains on the windows, with a matching tablecloth on the small, dining room table. Two, adequately sized bedrooms, with warm quilts and soft pillows, were welcoming and inviting. The bathroom had a sizeable shower, and the kitchen was surprisingly well stocked with everything needed for making delicious meals. At the back of the cabin, a door led out to a small deck and outer building that housed a washer and dryer, and had extra room for storage.

Once Michael had his bearings, he unloaded his supplies and settled in for the evening. Tomorrow, he'd go for a hike in the woods to scout out fallen trees, so he could build displays for his jewelry.

There were some finishing touches to be applied to his creations, and prayers yet to be said over his work. As he contemplated the future, a restorative sense of peace washed over him and he genuinely looked forward to what the days ahead would hold.

STRYKER

The man leaning against the side of the black pickup truck was dressed in black jeans, a black shirt, and wearing a black cap on his head. He had pulled over at a turnout along the creek to stretch his legs and to have a smoke. Pulling a pack of Camels from his pocket, he tapped out a cigarette and placed it between his teeth. Tearing off a match, with the flick of his wrist, the tiny matchstick sprung to life, but as he raised his hand to his mouth to light the tobacco, a gust of wind snuffed it out. He looked up just in time to see the taillights of a baby blue & white VW van sweep quickly past him. A dark shadow visibly passed over his face as he watched the van disappear around the bend.

Michael... you did make it after all...

His upper lip curled back as he struck another match, lighting the cigarette. He inhaled deeply and tossed the matchstick over his shoulder onto the ground.

I hate to disappoint you... correction... I look forward to disappointing you. Let's just see who has the last laugh here, my friend!

With a sneer on his chiseled face, the man in black walked back to the driver's door and jumped into the cab of the pickup. Revving the engine, he slid the truck into gear and trailed after the VW van.

Reflecting back on his visit to the city, he marveled at how easily things had gone for him. Doors just seemed to open wide, welcoming him to walk through them. He didn't have a bit of trouble securing a truck with a camper on the back. The special shipment he was expecting had arrived precisely on time at the airport that morning and everything had gone as smooth as silk. Display racks were waiting nearby with his name on them, at a distribution center, and were easy to purchase and load up. The magnetic logo signs for the sides of his truck had turned out better than he had expected and he knew that advertising would be the thing that made his endeavor a successful one. The camper on the back was spacious and it secured everything he needed for his special assignment.

He remembered seeing a campground at the lake. It would be an adequate place for him to set up camp for what he hoped would be a brief stay in Hicksville!

The Springtime Flower Festival would be happening in the very near future and he was excited to get things rolling. He was sure that his product would be a hot seller, once word spread like wildfire that he was in town. Suckers were a dime a dozen and he was good at luring them in.

Chloe. Such a beautiful name, such a dreary little town. Too bad the residents are just a bunch of simpletons. Correction... so GLAD... they are all just a bunch of simpletons! Come to me, little lambs... and let me give you eyes that see! Let me enlighten you...

Stomping on the gas, he was sure he could make the campground well before nightfall, but sometimes even the best made plans fail to succeed.

It was looking like a faulty gas gauge would prevent Stryker from reaching his destination before dark, and he beat the steering wheel with both hands as the truck he was driving sputtered into the meadow on the outskirts of Chloe.

"Perfect! Just what I was hoping for! Now, I can pitch my tent in the middle of this mosquito infested wasteland and hitchhike into town in the morning for gas! Ab-so-lute-ly PERFECT!!" he growled.

A blanket of biting mosquitos swarmed his truck, and a startled jackrabbit jetted for cover nearby.

Climbing out of the cab, Stryker kept the headlights on while he slapped mosquitos and dug into the back of the camper for his tent and sleeping bag. After locating them, he fumbled around, trying to figure out how to pitch the tent. He was no Boy Scout, and was too proud to ask the man at the store who had sold him the camping gear how to put the tent together. In the end, he found himself accidently snapping one of the tent poles in two.

"GREAT!"

Scrapping the tent, he threw his sleeping bag on the ground and crawled into it, but the buzzing insects, eager for a meal, were pushing the man in black to the breaking point.

Stryker jumped out of the sleeping bag and stormed his way back to the pickup. Ripping open the door, he began frantically searching the glove compartment for insect repellant. It didn't take long for him to realize that he had forgotten to purchase bug spray.

"REALLY?!!!"

Abandoning the idea of a night spent fighting sleep beneath the stars, he remained in the cab of the truck and opted to muscle through till morning by curling up on the bench seat.

The buzzing continued, as a multitude of the tormenting predators had followed him inside the truck. He sat bolt upright, flipped on the inside cab light, and began swatting at as many of them as he could see. It was well after midnight before he pulled his shirt up over his head and gave up.

The following morning, Stryker looked into the rearview mirror and lost count after 26 bites on his face, neck and torso. His shirt had obviously failed to protect him from the onslaught in the night.

After climbing out of the truck, he stretched, rubbed a pulled muscle in his neck from sleeping at a bad angle, and scratched several of the red, itching bumps covering his skin. *Note to self, never trust a gas gauge and never, ever, go anywhere without insect repellant!*

His attention turned to the road when the sound of a rumbling farm truck filled with goats, came lumbering towards him. Stryker planted his feet in the middle of the blacktop, and waved his hands wildly in the air. The farmer's brakes screeched to a halt as he rolled down his window.

"Looks like you need some help, mister!"

"I do. I ran out of gas. Could you give me a lift into town?"

"I can, but you'll have to ride in the back with the goats. My front seat is full of milk bottles to be delivered to the market."

Eyeing the back, the stranded, mosquito bitten man decided that it would be better to ride with the goats, than to walk into town. Especially after the previous night's sleep!

With a nod of his head, Stryker frightened the goats as he crawled into the back of the hay strewn truck, and the smelly, filthy contents had him mumbling under his breath, "*Just great...*"

Once in town, Stryker brushed off the straw, before walking into Mathews' Hardware store. He needed to buy a gas can, insect repellant and a replacement tent pole.

Few words were exchanged between Fred Mathews and the edgy stranger. It was obvious that his latest customer wanted to get in and out of there as quickly as possible. Fred's friendly attempt at being helpful, to the man dressed entirely in black, was blatantly rejected and the speedy transaction that followed took place amidst deathly silence.

When the man exited the store, a shiver ran down Fred's spine. Returning to the task of restocking shelves, the store's owner tried to shake off the disturbing encounter, all the while, thinking... *they say it takes all kinds... but I'm not so sure about that one!*

After striking up a conversation with a young man filling up his car at the gas station, Stryker asked him for a ride back to his truck. The young man was heading that way and assured him that it would be no problem.

Once back at the meadow, Stryker emptied the fuel from the can into the tank, and tossed the empty can, the repellant, and tent pole, into the back of the camper. He then returned to the gas station, filled up the truck and spare gas can, and decided to make a brief stop at the grocery store for some supplies. From there, he would head to the campground.

When he finally arrived at the lake's camping area, Stryker was merrily greeted with a strong handshake and a big smile from Ranger Bud. His attempt to return the smile fell flat, and the campground manager wasted no time in swiftly assigning him a campsite and handing him a map.

Stryker was less than pleased when he realized that his camping spot was at the back of the campground, and within walking distance to the dumpster. When the wind shifted, he was treated to the stench of many a happy camper's, leftover trash! "Great! I probably should have purchased bear spray too, because THAT smells like it's right up their alley! And if that's dinner... what does that make me? Dessert?" "Looks like I'll be making another trip back to town," grumbled the not-so-happy camper.

FRIENDS, FOES, AND FLOWERS

Friday morning began with a breathtaking sunrise in a beautiful blue sky. With the bright sun shining, it was the perfect day to begin the festival.

"Bless my soul, Esther, what a beeeee-u-ti-ful day... and the weatherman says we can expect it to stay this way throughout the weekend! Isn't that terrific, Esther? Frieda Gayle's shortcake sure tastes better on a sunny day, don't ya think, Esther? It's gonna be a fantastic festival... I just know it!" beamed Mayor Fink.

"Shortcake... schmortcake! All I ever hear is talk about Frieda Gayle's shortcake! Is that all there is to talk about in this town? Truth be known... I've tasted better!" retorted the feisty secretary.

Esther spun around and marched her way to the ladies room in the courthouse. She had to take a moment to compose herself before setting out for the park. She never knew who she might run into and she certainly wanted to look her best. Like her mother always said, *"Look your best, feel your best!"*

Glancing in the mirror she admired her relatively smooth complexion. *Not too bad... for a girl up in her numbers!*

She tried taming her unruly, mouse brown hair by tightening her hairpins and securing the bun at the nape of her neck. For the final touch, she applied a fresh coat of Fire Truck Red lipstick. Her favorite color. With a twist of her pearls, she proclaimed to the mirror, "To the town park with you, Esther Mae Brumble!"

Stopping briefly at her office, she retrieved her purse, a notebook, a pen and her festival agenda. With a quick shout over her shoulder, she told the mayor she was on her way to the park to help set things up.

Keeping her eyes straight ahead at all times... *clickity clack... clickity clack...* went her heels as she marched down the brick sidewalk.

"No time to stop and talk. Small talk is for small people, as mother always said." *Clickity clack... clickity clack...*

When she turned the corner at Columbine Street, she was surprised to see that so much progress had been achieved without her. Glancing at her watch she verified that it was only 9:30. *They knew they were not supposed to begin setting up until 10:00! SHE was supposed to be the first one there! The nerve of them!!*

"Hello there, Ms. Esther!" waved Sheldon, the park's maintenance supervisor. He was busy touching up the paint on the welcome sign at the park's entrance. "Looks like we're going to have splendiferous weather this weekend!"

Esther breezed right past him with a half-smile barely moving her flaming Red Fire Truck, lips.

When she arrived at the tables beneath the pavilion, she tossed down her purse and flipped open her notebook. She'd stuck the pen over her ear before leaving her office, and it was difficult to remove from her hair-sprayed doo.

She noticed that the sand in the sandbox had been sifted and raked. Check! The playground equipment appeared to be in good working order. Check! The grass had been cut, raked, and the bushes trimmed. Check, check, check! The restrooms had a fresh coat of paint on the outside. Check! The inside of the women's restroom was sparkling clean, and she noticed a fresh coat of paint had been applied. Check, check! The men's bathroom... who cares. Check!

Outdoor pavilion... tables scrubbed, and concrete swept. Check, check! Barbeque grill? Barbeque grill??!! CAKED with crud! "SHEEEEEEEELDON!!!"

Sheldon ran as fast as he could with his paintbrush flinging paint along the way. "Ms. Esther! What's wrong? Did you see a snake?!!"

"No, Sheldon! Something worse!! Look at this grill... it's a filthy mess!!"

"Patience, dear woman, cleaning the cooker is next on my list. See here?" When Sheldon reached into his shirt pocket for his notes, paint flew through the air, splattering some of it on the end of Esther's nose.

"SHEEEEEEEELDON!!!"

"Sorry, Ms. Esther. Here, let me wipe that off for you!" He leaned forward, pulling a grimy bandana from a pocket in his overalls.

"STOP RIGHT THERE, SHELDON! You've done more than enough!" She held up both hands in front of her, warding him off. Spinning on her heel, she marched back as fast as she could to the women's restroom.

Michael drove his van through the park's entrance and smiled at the paint splattered man walking towards him.

"Good morning, sir. My name's Michael Rain and I've been assigned space 12-B?"

"Sure thing, Mr. Rain. 12-B's down past that clump of bushes on the right. Then, turn left and follow the yellow tape tied between the trees. I hung the numbers off the yellow tape. You'll see it."

"Thank you, Mister....?"

"Sheldon. Just Sheldon. Good luck to you, Mr. Rain!"

Michael found his designated space without trouble and proceeded to unload the back of the van. Intuitively, he felt eyes boring into his back. Upon turning, he acknowledged the source. *Stryker!*

Stryker was leaning up against a tree, smoking a Camel, when Michael's eyes met his. For a fraction of a second Michael saw fear flash through them, but Stryker quickly turned away to snuff out his cigarette on the tree. The man in black walked away without a word.

It was best for both of them, that they were not neighbors at the festival...

Michael snapped together the cube shaped tables that would hold his displayed jewelry. Next, he assembled the deep sky-blue awning that provided shade and protection from the elements.

Further down the row, Stryker was unloading his truck and putting together the framework for his cave-like booth. Heavy black canvas covered the top and wrapped around three sides. He attached mirrors on the inside walls with Velcro, and unrolled a large rubber mat to cover the grass within the cave.

Next, he ran extension cords and installed blacklights on retractable poles at each corner. In the center of the dark abyss, he placed several eyeglass displays that spun around easily. After they were arranged accordingly, he ripped open boxes to reveal his precious merchandise. Sunglasses... and not just your everyday type! His were sleek and stylish and were sure to *enlighten* the wearer.

Stryker stepped back and reached up to hang his sign on the front of the cave's entrance. In bold red & white print it read, *D. STRYKER'S, DARK EYES*. Beneath it, it read, *Shades that will keep them guessing...* The same logo was stuck on the outside of both doors of his pickup truck.

Meanwhile, Michael's space was coming together quite nicely. He'd covered the grass beneath his awning with a cotton-soft white rug. He positioned the cubes within the space accordingly, and placed the pine burl displays on top of the flat surfaces. The gnarled chunks of wood had been lightly sanded and polished with lemon oil. The natural contour of the burls offered hollows and outcroppings, perfect for cradling earrings and bracelets, and small golden nails were added to hang necklaces.

The necklaces. They were the most cherished pieces in his collection. A single raindrop shaped stone, suspended from a sky-blue silk cord, appeared to be floating, as it was difficult to figure out how it was attached to the cord. Pearlescent in nature, when sunlight hit the raindrops, they were almost iridescent. Each raindrop shimmered as if it were alive. It was hard to tell if the color actually changed in the light, or if your eyes were just playing tricks on you. Visually, each drop seemed to change from varying shades of blue, green, lavender, white and pink... but it was ever-so subtle.

Michael had also designed some that might appeal more to the male population, by suspending the raindrops from leather cords.

A single mirror rested upon the surface of one of the cubes. Michael believed in one-on-one attention with each patron.

Once everything was in place, he added the finishing touch. A simple sign hanging from above that read, *LOVE RAINS DOWN, by Michael Rain.*

It was well past lunch when Esther decided that the booths were looking satisfactory. All except for maybe Frieda Gayle's Strawberry Shortcake booth. The plastic flowers, the eyelet and rickrack ribbons, and the red & white checked plastic table cloths... would never measure up, in Esther's mind.

Sheldon, who happened to be standing nearby when Esther donned her white gloves for a health inspection, noticed that Esther's nose was slightly elevated. Hmmm...

"On with the inspection!"

She went to work scrutinizing Frieda Gayle's booth and eventually decided that it was just barely, "Good enough!"

Willow Sanders' booth, *Blossoms & Blooms,* was Esther's favorite. She was continually impressed with the arrangements Willow created. Her displays were set up, but the fresh flowers wouldn't arrive until the following morning. Willow would cut them from the field just after sunrise and place them in buckets of water. Jack always helped her load them into the back of old Buttercup, and he and Willow would drive them into town to the park. Once there, she would put together bouquets in pots, tin cans, and old wooden boxes. She had an antique wheel barrow placed at the front of her booth that would overflow with brightly colored flowers. Willow was never afraid to be creative. Last year she planted flowers in an old bedpan. Esther had to buy that one, because it reminded her of grandmother Brumble.

At five o'clock, on that Friday afternoon, Esther announced loudly, with a bullhorn provided by Sheldon, that the park was closed until eight o'clock the next morning.

"BE HERE AT EIGHT O'CLOCK SHARP! AND NOT ONE SECOND BEFORE!!" she bellowed.

SEIZE THE DAY

Bluegrass music could be heard from blocks away as the band played their hearts out beneath the wooden gazebo. Barefoot children, with sticky hands full of pink cotton candy, danced merrily around the bandstand. Artisans, painters, metal workers, photographers, you name it, they were all there, and the Springtime Flower Festival was off to a grand start!

Water was splashing wildly as local students waited patiently for their turn to dunk their school principal in the dunking tank. Frieda Gayle's wish was granted this year, with her Strawberry Shortcake stand being located not far from the Silent Auction. Cromwell, Fink's trusty canine, was a happy dog. He spent his day sniffing around between the *Shortcake Palace* and the *Barbeque Grill*. Cromwell was more than willing to be part of the cleanup committee.

Sheldon was wearing an apron and chef's hat, and was busy flipping burgers and hotdogs on the "Esther Approved...Up to Code... BBQ Grill." The Boy Scouts were selling ice cold drinks nearby, and their booth appeared fully staffed with several scouts in uniform, in attendance. The smoke from the grill had many of them hacking and coughing, but when the wind shifted their way, it was to be expected.

Further down the line, Henry and Jake Davis had a booth right next to Willow's *Blossoms & Blooms*. They built birdhouses, small tables, bookshelves and wooden toys for children. Willow thought that both men, and their creations, were absolutely charming and she was always happy to be located next to them. She loved helping the two woodworkers, and she offered them several pots of flowers to help brighten up their booth. She knew that flowers were a sure-fire way to catch the eye of each passer-by. Henry was grateful for her contribution, but would only agree, if she would accept his prized birdhouse in exchange. Willow said she had the perfect spot for it back at the cottage, and she'd cherish it!

Willow's smile brought much joy to the old man's heart. She reminded him a great deal of his daughter Stella, Jacob's mother. His dear sweet girl... lost to dreams of city lights and fame. It had been years since they'd received a postcard from California, and the phone calls ended way before then. Yes, it was good medicine to be next to Willow and her girls. He never mentioned it, but he secretly hoped that Jacob would notice Daisy and fall in love with her one day. He wanted Jacob to settle down with a local girl and live in the house on the lake. Daisy was perfect for him, in Henry's mind.

Just past the Silent Auction, were the Camp Fire Girls. Their fresh pies and baked goods were always popular with the crowd. Stacy Mathews, troop leader, along with her daughters and several others, were afraid they may run out of goodies before the day was through. This year's festival was proving to be bigger than ever.

The sack races, in full swing, were competently run by the High School Athletic Department. The *Hares*, were rewarded food and drink coupons, redeemable at all booths offering the like, and the

Tortoises, were given a consolation prize. Free face painting provided by the Chloe United Babysitter's Club. All participants were guaranteed a smiling face... even if it had to be painted on.

Fred Mathews and Calvin Bailey ran the Rubber Ducky Race. This year they had more ducks than ever before in the water. The winner of the race would be announced at the end of the day by Mayor MacFarland, and the *Pot-o-Gold* would be awarded.

The Spring Festival was going strong and the park was bustling from one end to the other with laughter and activity. Daniel Kramer was kept on his toes with Mayor MacFarland sending him to and fro, running errands. Fink always seemed to have a list of duties an arm long, for *Danny Boy!*

On the far side of the park, Stryker was restocking sunglasses when Daisy and Wallace happened to pass by his booth.

"Hey, look Dais. Cool sunglasses!"

Daisy stopped and looked them over. Selecting a midnight blue frame with mirrored lenses, she placed them on her face and turned towards one of the many mirrors. Wallace grabbed a similar pair that was charcoal gray in color, and did the same. Instantly, their faces seemed to transform.

Only Stryker noticed the expected lifting of their brows, and with a calculated smile, he said to them, "Who wouldn't want to look that cool?! Tell you what... I'm going to give you a 20% discount, because I know you'll be great advertisement!"

Wallace and Daisy stared at themselves in the mirror for the longest time.

"These are different from any sunglasses I've ever had. I think they make me feel like a super hero! I bet I could drive a motorcycle through the canyon going 100 miles per hour!" exclaimed Wallace.

"Yeah, I'm feeling like anything's possible with these on. I bet I could climb up a sheer rock face without a rope, and I don't even like climbing rocks..." professed Daisy.

"We'll take them!" they said in unison.

With their *"Dark Eyes"* in place, they continued weaving their way through the crowd. The festival was appearing to be a lot more fun with new shades on.

Stopping at Michael's booth, they simultaneously pushed their glasses up on top of their heads, so that they could see the jewelry more clearly.

"LOVE RAINS DOWN... by Michael Rain. Interesting!" said Daisy.

"Wow, Wallace, these necklaces are extraordinary." She plucked one from the display and held it up in the sunlight. It spun and danced at the end of the silken blue cord and Daisy did a double take. She could have sworn that she saw something within the raindrop. A bird, maybe?

Michael handed Wallace a slightly larger raindrop that hung from a dark leather cord.

"What kind of stone is this?" asked Wallace. "I've never seen anything like it."

Michael answered him by saying, "It comes from a faraway place. Please, take them both. They're a gift... from me to you..."

Daisy put hers around her neck, and Wallace followed suit. An immediate sense of peace, radiated through the both of them.

"Wow... awesome! Thank you so much for these, Mr. Rain. We'll treasure them..." said Daisy as she turned towards Michael.

"You two are more than welcome. Have a blessed day..."

Michael's eyes reflected a gentleness from within, and his jewelry seemed to mirror that attribute, giving a measure of it away with each raindrop.

Derek Cyrus breezed right past the trio, never looking their way, but Michael noticed the direction in which the young man was headed.

When Derek reached the sunglass booth, he immediately went for a shiny black pair with doubly dark lenses. Putting them on, he looked briefly into the mirror and turned towards Stryker.

"How much? I'll give you thirty bucks. It's all I got..." said Derek.

"Sold!"

Stryker took the boys money and shot a quick glance towards his eyebrows. *Yep... he's hooked!*

Derek turned and walked away, never looking back. He hadn't met up with Shayne yet and he was eager to find her.

Shayne was standing by the Dunking Tank, watching the principal get his dues. Derek nudged her with his shoulder to get her attention. She instantly noticed that her friend was sporting a new pair of shades and she immediately said, "I want a pair! Where did you get them?!"

"Come on... I'll show you."

Upon arriving at the booth, they had to wait their turn, as quite the crowd had gathered to try on sunglasses.

Shayne noticed that the sunglasses weren't the only good-looking thing to admire in the booth. The guy selling them was not so bad looking himself.

"Hi there. Are you from around here?" she flashed him a sassy smile.

"I might be from around here, pretty lady, but I'll bet your daddy doesn't let you out of his sight very often."

"Oh, him. He let's me run my own life. He trusts me..." she replied confidently.

"Here, try this pair on." He handed her a deep crimson red pair, of a sleek design. She placed them on her face and turned towards the nearest mirror available. The corners of her mouth turned up ever so slightly as her eyebrows lifted.

"I'll take them. I don't care what they cost."

Stryker's cold smile never reached his eyes as he took the girl's money.

"Have a nice day, little lady..." he said as he bowed, tipping an imaginary hat.

Shayne pushed the glasses up onto the bridge of her nose and turned and walked away knowing full well that he was watching her go. Something compelled her to look back over her shoulder and when she did, his wicked grin made her smile.

Claire was ready for a break from the Camp Fire booth so she slipped away quietly when no one was looking. She wanted to get lost in the crowd. She wasn't good at talking to people and her face hurt from trying to smile as she sold baked goods. Most people knew that she was painfully shy and they respected her space, but there were always a few who never hesitated to tease and taunt her. If she were brave, she would wear a T-shirt that said, "I'm Shy, Don't Ask Why!" but that, of course would just draw attention, and she wasn't brave.

Passing by Michael's booth, the raindrop necklaces stopped her in her tracks. She couldn't take her eyes off of them. Carefully, lifting one from the display, she dangled it in front of her face.

"Is that a dove flying inside of it?" she whispered to herself.

A gentle voice responded, "Exactly right."

Claire jumped slightly and looked up into the warmest pair of brown eyes that she had ever seen.

"Oh..." she said.

"My name is Michael, and I would be honored if you would accept that necklace as a gift. It compliments the beautiful color of your eyes and you'd be doing me a favor if you'd wear it. The festival will be ending and everything must go."

"Well... if you're sure..."

"I'm sure. I'd be honored if you'd agree to take it."

She slipped it over her head and said, "Well then, thank you. I will treasure it."

As she walked away, she thought she heard him say, "God bless you, Claire..." but that was silly. How would he know her name?

As Claire headed back to continue her duties with the Camp Fire Girls, she happened to pass by the sunglass booth. Feeling eyes boring into her soul, a shiver ran down her spine.

He was dressed in black, and when their eyes locked, she grabbed the raindrop hanging from her neck and dropped her eyes towards the ground. Cutting a wide swath around him, she picked up her pace. As her heart raced within her, she stepped behind a tree to catch her breath before returning to her work. Holding the raindrop helped to calm her down, and she was grateful for the nice man in the jewelry booth.

When Max showed up at Henry and Jake's booth, Jake asked his grandpa if he'd mind if he took a break. Henry told him that it was perfectly fine with him.

The two friends decided to take a walk around the park, and Jacob skidded to a stop when his eyes were drawn to sunlight reflecting off of something. Upon close inspection, he was intrigued by the raindrop hanging from the dark leather cord, and was pleasantly surprised when the maker of it wouldn't let him pay for it. *Nice guy!*

Max stood several feet away, barely making eye contact with Michael. He nodded at him, but didn't get close enough to see what he was selling. He was more interested in buying a pair of sunglasses like Wallace Kramer's. Eager to locate the sunglass booth, Max urged Jacob to hurry up.

Max and Jake both tried on a pair of sunglasses and both of them bought them, instantly. Stryker smiled as the two walked away talking about whiskey and a mountaintop.

Derek and Shayne had separated for a while after lunch. He was walking at a fast pace trying to find her again when he literally bumped into Michael.

"Sorry, dude..." he said as he tried to move around him.

"Wait! Do you have a moment?" Michael said to the retreating boy's back. Derek stopped and turned towards the stranger.

Michael reached into his shirt pocket and pulled out a dark leather cord. "This is for you. No charge. I'm almost done here, and I want you to have it."

Derek started to shake his head, but after lifting his sunglasses up, something stopped him when he glanced down at the stone suspended from the cord.

"What's it made of? It's kinda weird. Weird in a good way though..." he said as he stared at the raindrop on the cord. When

Derek looked up into the stranger's eyes, he felt a sense of peace come over him.

"It comes from a faraway place... but please, take it. It's yours."

Derek smiled a half smile and thanked him as he walked away.

As the festival wound down and the crowd showed signs of thinning, the hardy gathered at the flower draped stage. Mayor MacFarland and Esther Brumble had remained front and center all day, making announcements with the faulty P.A. system, but the festival was officially coming to an end.

In wrapping up, Esther awarded Candy Anderson the Pot-o-Gold from the Rubber Ducky Race winnings. The Silent Auction participants were given their prized items, in exchange for the money they had agreed to, and Mayor Fink gave a long-winded speech thanking everyone... and then some.

Percy Taylor, resident journalist, scribbled notes for tomorrow's writeup in Chloe's one and only newspaper... *The Blue Sage News & Review*.

The following morning, those that had participated in making it all happen would gather up at Charlie's Coffee Cup & Café to relive the previous day's events, and to share ideas for next year's festival.

ARE WE THERE YET?

Dax Sherman was leaning back against the school bus, wearing faded blue jeans, a white long-sleeved T-shirt, hiking boots, and a baseball cap. He was looking down at his clipboard, going over his notes to make sure he wasn't forgetting something, when Naomi walked up to him.

"Miss Trent! You're here early!" Dax couldn't help but to notice her outfit. She was wearing something you'd expect to see in Africa on Safari; khaki cargo pants, a khaki shirt, snake boots, topped off with a pith helmet on her head.

"... and might I add, nice outfit?!"

Naomi blushed, "What... this old thing? My daddy used to take our family to Africa every other year and this is what we always wore." Tugging on her sleeve with one hand she popped the top of her helmet with the other. "The fabric breathes, provides UV protection and is very comfortable. Daddy said that you never know when something might fall from a tree and land on your head. He taught us to be prepared."

Covering his mouth with his hand, Dax suppressed a laugh by forcing a cough. "Yes, it's important to be prepared! Speaking of which, Louella was here at 4:00 this morning, preparing sack lunches in the cafeteria. Would you mind bringing them out so they can be loaded on the bus? Mr. Graves is driving and we'll make sure to load the luggage first so that the lunches will be easy to get to when we stop."

"Absolutely! Is there anything else I can do for you? I mean the kids... I mean... to help?" Her blush only deepened.

"No, I think we're good. Just drop off your gear on the ground near the storage compartment and we'll take it from there. I'll send some of the boys to help you. The Boy Scouts donated sodas and bottled water, leftover from the festival, and the ice chests will be heavy."

"Right-o!" Naomi saluted her handsome co-worker, knocking her pith helmet off in the process. When she accidently kicked it, sending it sliding across the pavement, Dax stifled another chuckle.

Sleepy teenagers began arriving shortly thereafter, dragging suitcases, duffle bags, sleeping bags and pillows. Derek was the first one to walk up to Mr. Sherman.

"Hey, thanks for the sleeping bag and stuff. It was right where you said it would be."

"You're welcome! Say, could you grab Jake and go help Miss Trent in the cafeteria? Our lunches and the ice chests need to be hauled out here so we can load them on the bus."

"Will do, Mr. Sherman." He dropped his gear and went to find Jake.

Dax watched him go. There was something special about that kid. He'd had a hard knock life and it just never seemed fair. He knew that the tide could turn for Derek, and he felt responsible to help him. Dax would not be where he was today, if it hadn't been for a hand up from one of his high school teachers. He'd always be grateful and paying it forward was never a question.

Camp counselors were arriving as well, and the activity and noise level was beginning to rise. Dax methodically doled out orders to various students and counselors, and necessary supplies were hauled over to the bus. He and Mr. Graves had it all loaded into the storage compartment just as Derek, Jake, and Miss Trent showed up with the food and drinks. Perfect timing.

Mr. Sherman whistled over the idling bus, getting everyone's attention.

"When I call your name, make sure you've got everything you need for the ride up the mountain... then climb aboard! Once you are on the bus, you will not be getting off of it until instructed to do so! I repeat! Once on... stay on!! Do you understand?!"

A collective, "Yes, Mr. Sherman!" was uttered as eyes rolled in true teenaged fashion.

"What if we need to pee? I mean... use the facilities?" squawked a boy from the back of the crowd.

"Go now, but make it snappy! We need to get this show on the road!"

Mr. Sherman stood by the door of the big yellow bus calling off names, while Miss Trent counted each one as they entered and were seated. In the end, 54 students and 10 faculty members were loaded up, and ready to go.

Mr. Graves slammed the outside compartment door and climbed up into the driver's seat. Shutting the main door, he released the air brakes with a loud Pfffffffffftttttttt...!!

"Soaring Eagle Lodge, here we come!"

As the bus was turning to exit the parking lot of the school, Wallace Kramer piped up from the back, "Are we there yet?!!" Laughter followed, along with pillows thrown in his direction.

The winding road carried them along the creek and through the canyon for almost two hours. Eventually, they made a right turn, crossing over Blue Sage Creek, via a black metal bridge. From there, the road continued to twist and turn before cutting between the mountains.

The happy travelers stopped at a campground along the way to stretch their legs and visit the outhouses. There was an artesian spring nearby and everyone was encouraged to wash their hands before receiving their bagged lunch. They were hoping to spend only 30-40 minutes there, so there was a lot of scrambling to get food and drink, and a good spot at a picnic table.

Derek and Shayne opted to sit apart from the group, by choosing to plop down on the ground beneath a tall pine tree. Both were wearing the sunglasses they'd purchased at the festival on Saturday, and the conversation between them was minimal. Any other time they would have been chattering up a storm, but not today. *Dark eyes concealed dark thoughts, perhaps?*

Claire Mathews was silently nibbling on her mystery meat and cheese sandwich when she happened to glance their way. She noticed the dark sunglasses along with the odd look on their faces. A shiver ran down her spine and goose bumps covered both arms. Subconsciously, she reached for the raindrop hanging from the silk cord around her neck.

"Ok, everyone! Hustle up! Garbage goes in the trash cans, and drinks are not allowed on the bus... so drink up!"

Once again, Dax pulled out his clipboard and began calling off names, Miss Trent took a head count, and everyone loaded back up to continue the journey.

From the campground, the going got a lot slower. The road consisted of a series of switchbacks and sharp turns as the lumbering bus maneuvered its way up the steep incline. They were still in the same mountain range as their beloved Mount Chloe, but Soaring Eagle Lodge was three quarters of the way up, tucked in on the backside of the mountain. The view from above was absolutely beautiful for as far as the eye could see, and as they neared their destination, excitement began to build.

Thaddeus Barron was expecting the bus to arrive around 2:00 that afternoon, and true to form, Mr. Graves brought the bus to a halt in front of the lodge at precisely 1:59. After setting the emergency brake, the bus door opened and the driver was once again, happy to see his old friend. He'd been driving the bus for the senior class camping trip for the past 15 years, and it tended to be one of the highlights of the year for him.

A few people commented on the lingering aroma of hot brakes and burning rubber. It was to be expected though, as the climb up the mountain was always an arduous and challenging one. Eventually, the noxious smell dissipated and fresh mountain air became the topic that replaced it.

"Ok, everyone! Listen up! Mr. Barron has been kind enough to post the cabin assignments ahead of time on the bulletin board inside the lodge. Please, take turns reading it! If you need to 'visit the facilities' they're located in the bathhouses, between the main building and the cabins. I'd like a few of you boys to volunteer to help unload the gear and supplies. Once everything is off of the bus, and you've obtained your cabin numbers, grab your things and go get settled in. Each cabin holds six students and one adult. Ok... get going! We meet back at the lodge at 4:30 sharp!!"

Dax was hopeful that this group of students would prove to be respectful, as well as good listeners. Watching them head for the main building, he knew they were all grateful to be breathing sweet mountain air after the long ride on the school bus. He certainly was. Chattering voices, giggles, and a few grumbles, accompanying them on their way to learning their fate, brought a smile to his face. It was going to be a good week. He just knew it.

Ten minutes later, Dax was still standing outside near the lodge when Wallace Kramer's head popped up in the empty bus.

Stifling a yawn, the boy rubbed his sleepy eyes and squawked, "Are we there yet?"

CABIN LIFE

The handcrafted log cabins were nestled beneath stately pines and swaying aspens. Thaddeus and his younger brother Tobias, designed and built them with the purpose in mind of hosting retreats for those longing to spend time up in the mountains. Soon after construction was completed, Tobias became a missionary and ended up living all over the world, helping those less fortunate, while Thaddeus, vowed to live on the mountain until Jesus came to take him home.

Each cabin contained three sets of log bunkbeds, perfect for the students, and a single twin log bed for the supervising adult. Steamer trunks were situated beside them for storage, but also doubled as nightstands for the bottom bunks. A small table with a reading lamp and two chairs, placed beneath one of the windows, offered the best spot for reading and writing.

With red & white gingham curtains dressing each window, and brightly colored throw rugs covering the hardwood floors, the accommodations were cozy and inviting.

As charming as the cabins were, Claire Mathews countenance sank when she saw that Shayne Darby was to be one of her cabin mates. That uneasy feeling that she experienced when the bus stopped for lunch, was still lingering. Shayne and Derek looked extremely agitated and almost evil with their dark sunglasses on. They were never Claire's favorite people, but today was eye-opening to say the least. As for Shayne, her Irish temper turned her into a bully sometimes, and in the past, truth be known, she'd never been very friendly to Claire.

Why couldn't Daisy Wilson be in my cabin? At least she's nice, and oftentimes, thoughtful... well, except when Wallace is around. He doesn't always bring out the best in her... but Daisy would at least be able to disarm Shayne when her mood takes a vile turn for the worse!

Deep in thought, Claire unrolled her sleeping bag and began arranging it on the last available bottom bunk.

Everyone jumped, when Shayne Darby loudly entered the cabin, kicking the door shut behind her with her foot. Her arms were loaded with all of her things, and Claire noticed that those awful sunglasses were still perched on her nose.

Dropping her gear in the middle of the floor, she stated, "I'm here... and not so fast, darlin'! That bottom bunk has my name written all over it, mouse girl! Move your crap! Now!"

Claire looked to her other roommates for moral support, but they all turned their backs on the scene and busied themselves with unpacking. Claire quickly yanked her sleeping bag and pillow off of the bed and moved them to the farthest available upper bunk. Away from the beastly girl.

"Great choice, Minnie!" smirked the bully in residence.

Thanks for nothing, Beth Anne... Martha... Suzanne... and Taylor. Will I ever have a friend besides Dr. Morton? I wish I could have smuggled him into my duffle bag...

Before tears could form in Claire's eyes, revealing her emotional state, Miss Trent entered the cabin like a ray of sunshine.

"Hello, girls! Guess who's been assigned your cabin? Yep! Just little old me... and we are going to have the best time!"

Claire heaved a huge sigh of relief. Miss Trent had always been sweet and understanding towards her, and Claire knew that Shayne wouldn't get away with being cruel to others, with Miss Trent around.

Further down the path, Cabin #4 was off to a great start. Daisy was thrilled to find out that Mrs. Welch, her 11th grade calculus teacher, who she really liked, was their cabin supervisor. And her cabin mates; Lisa, Fran, Brianna, Ava and Holly, were all nice enough. Maybe, just maybe, this camping trip would prove to be better than even she could have imagined!

The cabins housing the boys were somewhat separated from those housing the girls. Max and Jake were happy to find out that they would be in the same cabin, and their other roommates were tolerable, which was a plus. Wallace was a nerd, but harmless. Tommy and Aaron, twin brothers, got along with everyone, and Derek was a bit of a wild card, but he mostly kept to himself.

After all of them had chosen bunks and settled in, Mr. Sherman walked in. Derek was still wearing his sunglasses when a scowl formed beneath them. Through darkly veiled eyes, his thoughts simmered.

Sherman! Of all the luck! He may be nice sometimes... but this is going to cramp my style. He won't let us get away with anything!

Before Mr. Sherman could get a word out, Wallace accidently tripped and landed on Derek's foot with the heel of his boot.

Derek jumped up immediately and grabbed Wallace by his shirt collar, twisting it in his fist. Wallace gasped for air as Derek practically lifted him off the floor by his shirt.

Max yelled, "Fight!!"

The "fight" ended quickly when Mr. Sherman grabbed Derek by the arm and said, "Drop him!!"

Derek's elbow flew up and popped Dax in the mouth, causing his bottom lip to instantly swell and bleed. Derek's glasses flew off of his face and slid beneath the bunk when Wallace took a swipe at him, cuffing him under the chin.

"That's enough! I mean it!! Now... you! Derek! Have a seat on your bed... and you, Wallace! Sit down at that table!" He shoved the two boys in opposite directions.

When they saw Mr. Sherman's nostrils flaring, they knew that he meant business! Wallace immediately apologized, and Derek said, "Yeah... what he said..." while Dax, just stared at the two boys.

Dabbing at his bloody lip, Mr. Sherman continued, "Listen up! Mr. Arnold drove his pickup truck up here for this very reason, and he is more than willing to haul your sorry butts off of this mountain! Do you understand me?!"

"Yes Sir..." replied a repentant Wallace Kramer.

"Yes... Sir." echoed a not so convincing Derek Cyrus.

"Alright! There will be no more fighting. I'm giving you both one more chance... but if you so much as make one wrong move, you're out of here! This camping trip is a privilege and I'd appreciate it if you'd recognize that fact! Am I understood?!"

"Yes Sir," they replied in unison.

"Now, get cleaned up and get to the lodge. You've got ten minutes! Hustle up!!"

He could hear them scramble as he exited the cabin to go to the bathhouse to wash his hands and clean up his lip.

Derek crawled under his bunk to retrieve his sunglasses. He dusted them off and put them back on his face. Glaring at Wallace, he thought... *Lots of luck to you, nerd boy! That's right! This matter is nowhere near being finished...*

When Wallace saw Derek glaring at him, he suddenly broke out in a cold sweat. Compelled to hide behind his own pair of dark shades, he quickly dug them out of his backpack and put them on. *I can stare right back at you... you, worthless piece of humanity!*

Aaron broke the tension by stating, "We'd better get going, or we'll all be late! I think it's safe to say we've seen enough of the wrath of Sherman for one day!"

The boys marched out of the cabin single file with Derek bringing up the rear.

SOARING EAGLE LODGE

The open beamed ceiling inside Soaring Eagle Lodge was a magnificent work of art. The entire surface was covered in wide, white pine planks, and the beams, golden honey in color, were oversized knotty pine logs. What made the beams so special were the carvings, depicting a variety of local wildlife. Upon close inspection, you'd find a bighorn sheep, a mountain lion, a white-tailed deer, a young bull elk, a moose, a mother grizzly bear with twin cubs, and a pair of hawks flying overhead.

The walls were covered in white pine planks as well, and a large, native rock fireplace, ran from floor to ceiling at the far end of the lodge. A heavy mantle stretched across the rock wall, just above the firebox. It too, was exquisitely made from yet another knotty pine log, and was adorned with additional carvings. There were rainbow trout, raccoons, chipmunks, cottontail rabbits, a beaver, a badger, and a small bobcat. Highlighted in the center of the mantle was a majestic eagle in flight. Thaddeus was the artisan behind the craftsmanship and his work was breathtaking to say the least.

The lodge was reminiscent of an art gallery, displaying large black and white photos chronicling the building of Soaring Eagle Lodge and the cabins. On several walls, paintings and photographs, featuring local artists, could also be enjoyed. Groves of pines and aspens, wildflowers growing around lichen covered boulders, wildlife in its natural habitat, and mountains at sunset, were just a few of the paintings to be admired. Stunning photographs of waterfalls, winding trails and high mountain lakes, also graced the walls of the lodge.

The floors throughout the main lodge were made of natural slate, and the furnishings were built from local timber. There was a designated area for dining, and a large buffet table along one wall for serving meals. Long wooden tables with benches were lined up in rows in the middle of the room, perfect for guests to enjoy their meals. Canning jars filled with water and wildflowers were placed on the tabletops, adding a special touch to the dining experience.

Casual lounging was arranged near the fireplace and brightly colored Native American throw rugs added warmth to the floor. There were four large leather oversized couches, and several pairs of leather easy chairs with ottomans, on the far end. Side tables were situated between the chairs, and coffee tables were placed between the facing couches. Over the years, many a story had been shared and conversation flowed easily in the comfort of Soaring Eagle Lodge. Especially, on cold nights in front of a roaring fire.

On the day of their arrival, at 4:30 sharp, the students met up outside the lodge. Since the weather was mild, they were instructed to go around the building and down a short path to an outdoor amphitheater. Once there, they found seats made from a combination of logs and slate, arranged in half circles, built on several different levels, descending down toward a flat staging area.

Behind the center stage, a babbling brook gently tumbled along. On the opposite side of the water, there was a beautiful grove of aspens and a pine forest beyond that. The sound of the brook was soothing, and the scent of pine, carried on the slight breeze, was intoxicating.

Mr. Sherman, Miss Trent and the camp counselors stood together at center stage, as Mr. Sherman called for everyone's attention.

"Take a seat please and listen up! I'd like to start by asking for a warm round of applause for our gracious host, Mr. Thaddeus Barron! Because of his hard work, we get to enjoy the next week here in this unbelievably gorgeous setting!"

The sound of clapping hands put a warm smile on the big bear of a man's face and he responded by saying, "The pleasure is all mine! Please... Enjoy!"

Someone in the crowd hollered, *"Thank you Thaddeus!!"* Mr. Sherman then proceeded to ask that everyone address their host as *"Mr. Barron,"* since formality and manners would go a long way!

Over the next 30 minutes Mr. Sherman, Miss Trent and the other supervising adults went over lists of expectations and goals that were to be met during the week to follow. Each day they would be participating in various group activities and Miss Trent tried to reassure them that it would... *"all be a lot of fun!"* They'd also be allowed some free time to do as they chose, within limits. Swimming, reading, journaling, sketching, napping, and short hikes around the lake, were among a few of the things that were permissible.

The not-so-fun stuff would include taking turns washing dishes, wiping off tables, hauling in firewood, sweeping and mopping floors, cleaning the bathhouses and taking out the trash. There was a list of assigned duties posted on the bulletin board in the lodge for their *viewing pleasure!* It would be *"character building,"* according to Mr. Sherman.

Wallace Kramer's eyes lit up when he heard the news. He was excited about free time! He would be free to collect water samples, catch bugs and butterflies... and Daisy Wilson!

Orientation ended when dinnertime arrived. At 5:30, Cookie hammered away on the triangle outside the kitchen door, announcing that dinner was ready.

Mr. Sherman had to explain what the sound of the triangle meant to them, and hungry campers shouted with glee as they scrambled back up the steps, and raced to the lodge.

Dinner that first night consisted of fried chicken, potatoes and gravy, tossed green salad, and fresh baked bread with butter. For dessert they could have fresh apple pie alamode or chocolate cake with strawberry ice cream. Everyone was in agreement that the food at Soaring Eagle Lodge was outstanding. Thankfully, there were no chores required on day one, and it would have been fruitless to ask them to help as they were too excited to think about responsibilities.

When the sun went down behind the mountain, a bonfire was lit by the lake and all campers were happy to sit around it. Thaddeus and two of his employees played guitars, leading the group in song. They played mostly bluegrass and mountain songs, but they also threw in a few Irish tunes and several traditional campfire songs.

Naomi Trent could not contain her joy when a lively jig began. She tossed her pith helmet, as if it were a frisbee, and it landed beneath a nearby tree. She kicked up her heels and grabbed Dax's hand, begging him to join her. The kids all laughed, and this time it was Mr. Sherman's turn to blush. He was a good sport though, blaming his flaming red cheeks on the hot bonfire.

When the logs turned to embers beneath the starry night sky, Thaddeus shared a ghost story that began with... *"It was a black, and storm ravaged night!"* ending with, *"... and they were never seen or heard from... ever again!"* After that, he said, *"Pleasant dreams, campers!"* ... and the counselors escorted their charges back to their assigned cabins.

There was just enough time to brush teeth and use the restrooms before turning in, as everyone had to be back and in their sleeping bags before ten o'clock. The lodge and cabins were all powered by a generator and at ten o'clock sharp, the lights went out.

LIFE LESSONS

Shayne sat up abruptly in bed and smacked her head on the upper bunk in the process. *"Ouch!!! And are those bagpipes that I'm hearing??"*

Rubbing the sleep from her eyes, and the knot, forming on her forehead, she climbed out of her sleeping bag and shuffled to the window. Pushing back the curtains, she peered out into the semi-darkness and sure enough, she hadn't been dreaming. There, sauntering amongst the cabins, in full kilt, playing the bagpipes, was Thaddeus Barron.

"Is there anything that guy can't play?" she said to no one in particular.

Cabin lights began popping on like fireflies around the camp, reminding Shayne to reach out to flip theirs on. She turned back around to face her bunk and noticed from the corner of her eye that Claire was slowly emerging from her bag. Shayne chuckled, telling her that she looked like, "a turtle poking its head out of its shell."

Claire smiled slightly, and bravely responded, "I think I'd enjoy being a turtle today, instead of a mouse!"

"Ok Minnie, fair enough. Today, you can be Turtle Girl."

Claire retreated back into her sleeping bag, proud of her brief moment of boldness. That tiny spark of hope... thinking that her nemesis might lay off of her for even one day... was encouraging.

Door hinges and screen doors were squeaking and slamming as sleepy campers went to and fro between their cabins and the bathhouses. Derek proclaimed that it was still, "dark thirty," but if you asked Mr. Sherman, it was fifteen minutes until breakfast. He told the boys that he expected them to be at the lodge before Cookie rang the triangle, so they had better hustle up. Being early rather than late, was a good habit to get into, and he told them that it was a life lesson that was certain to help them in the future.

"Breakfast... at 6:30?! Who thinks that's a great idea?" squawked a grouchy Max.

"I'm guessing... the Irish Rooster?" replied Jake. "Or is that the Scottish Rooster?"

Jacob Davis was used to getting up at the crack of dawn. Henry instilled that practice in him, early on. His grandpa was not a young man anymore and the lake house had plenty of chores to attend to, before and after school. Weekends, too. Maxwell Darington, on the other hand, was a very entitled rich kid who was used to sleeping in whenever possible.

"Somebody better wake up Wallace," said one of the twins.

"I don't think he'd wake up if firecrackers went off on our cabin doorstep," said the other.

Derek grabbed the corner of Wallace's sleeping bag and jerked him off the top bunk, causing him to land on the cold floor with a loud... THUNK!

"Hey!!! What the heck are you doing?!" cried a bruised Wallace. He sat up in his sleeping bag, rubbing his right hip and shoulder.

"Rise & shine, Wally! Daylight's burning... according to Mr. Sherman!"

Wallace crawled out and stood up.

"Now, that's a picture!" Derek pointed his finger and laughed at the boy in the white vee neck T-shirt, and the way too small, tighty whities.

"Don't dilly-dally, Wally-Wally! If you're late for breakfast you'll probably go hungry! Sherman will see to that. To teach you a real... *life lesson*!"

The boys chuckled, as they looked forward to that first meal of the day.

With breakfast on her mind, Daisy literally ran into Derek when she flew out of her cabin door.

"Sorry, Derek. I didn't see you there... and I'm starving!" smiled the sunny girl with the long blonde hair.

Grinning back, he replied, "Not a problem. You can bump into me anytime!"

Shayne overheard Derek flirting with Daisy, and it surprised her that she didn't like the sound of it. Derek had always held the "friend card," but this morning, was she second guessing her game?

Derek was following behind Daisy when Shayne caught up to him.

"I thought we were going to walk to breakfast together?" After putting her sunglasses on, she snapped, "...or did you just forget to wait for me?!"

"Sorry, Shayne. I thought you'd be the first one in line at the serving table."

"Are you calling me fat?! Do you think I'd knock down everyone in my path... on the way to a stale biscuit?!" questioned the furious girl. "Oh, wait a minute... that was DAISY who knocked YOU down. My bad!"

Daisy stopped in her tracks and spun around to face her down.

"No, Shayne, Derek was just kind enough to break my fall when I tripped on my way out the door. You gotta a problem with that?" Daisy was also wearing her sunglasses that morning, and turning towards Derek she continued, "Thank you for rescuing a damsel in distress, kind sir!"

Without a glance back at Shayne, Daisy spun back around and quickly left the fuming girl behind.

"The NERVE of that little twit! Who does she think she is?!"

Derek pulled his sunglasses from his pocket and put them on.

"Lay off, Shayne. They're all just pawns in the game. You'll get your chance to retaliate."

Cookie was ringing the triangle as the pair strolled casually to the lodge.

After breakfast was devoured, those with assigned chores got to work. The rest of the students returned to their respective cabins to retrieve notebooks and pens. They had been instructed to find a quiet spot in the outdoor amphitheater or near the lake or in the nearby woods, to mandatorily write for 30 minutes in their journals. Many of them chose the lake as they were eager to see it in the daylight.

Derek and Shayne opted for the woods closest to the cabins. They felt lazy after the big meal they'd just consumed, so they didn't feel like venturing far. Everyone was told to write about their first impression of Soaring Eagle Lodge, and about the nature that surrounded it. Mr. Sherman would sound an elk bugle when the 30 minutes were up, and they were all expected to gather at the amphitheater at that time. By then, the *worker bees* should be finished with their chores, they could rejoin the group, but would be required to write in their journals during free time.

After a brief announcement, groups of six were formed and the students were each given a handout explaining the task they'd be performing that day. Some would take a walk in the woods, examining the ecosystem, and others would collect leaves, pine cones and insects. Bird watching was also on the list of things to experience. The counselors headed up the activities and lessons, but sunshine and fresh air was the bonus that made it all the more enjoyable.

They were given an hour of free time before lunch, and the afternoon was filled with storytelling, by local native, Running Deer. His stories were fascinating, and it was amazing to watch how he captivated his listeners in the telling. He was a full-blooded Shoshone Indian who would also be teaching them to weave baskets out of willows, later in the week.

When the sun dipped down and the moon rose high up in the night sky, they were taught a lesson in astronomy. Telescopes were arranged on the deck of the lodge, allowing the students the opportunity to take a closer look at planets, stars and constellations. Soon, this activity became a favorite of many.

After "lights out," a few boys in the cabin next door to Mr. Sherman's cabin, attempted to sneak out in the night. Running Deer happened to be making the rounds, as unbeknownst to them, he had volunteered to be the lookout for *unsuspecting escapees*. They were caught in the act and escorted back to their cabin. The next morning, they were made to stand in front of their classmates to confess their sin. Mr. Sherman said they would be forgiven this time, but anyone thereafter who thought that they could get away with sneaking out, would be sent home immediately. No more exceptions! Flashlights were to be used by counselors to escort those needing bathroom breaks in the night, but other than that, when the lights went out, everyone was expected to remain in their bunks.

The following morning, after their daily wakeup call and breakfast, the students were once again instructed to find a quiet place to write in their journals. Wallace Kramer thought it would be the perfect time to try out the *Love Potion,* that he'd concocted at home before coming to camp.

In his front right pocket, he carried a small vial filled with the magical cologne that was sure to send Daisy Wilson flying into his arms. He hid behind a tree while he spied on Daisy and Claire. They sat Indian style with wildflowers in their hair, in a grove of aspens, and were steadily writing in their notebooks. They were completely unaware of his presence.

Wallace unscrewed the cap on the vial and poured some of the liquid into his palm. He splashed some on his face and arms, and returned the half empty vial to his pocket. When he stepped out from behind the tree, the girls couldn't see him yet. A sudden gust of wind lifted Daisy's hair from around her face and a few of the flowers took flight. Her golden tresses were floating above her head, like an angel's halo, and Wallace couldn't keep his eyes off of her.

While staring at both of them, he noticed that Daisy and Claire had tipped their noses up at the same time. They were positioned downwind from the lovestruck boy, and in unison they chimed, "Is that a skunk?!" "Jinx, you owe me a Coke!!"

Wallace jumped back behind the tree, sniffed his arm, and ran back to the bathhouse. He wasn't sure if there was enough soap in the dispenser at the sink to reverse the magic, but he certainly hoped so!

So much for love...

THE JOURNEY BEGINS

Fundraisers were held throughout the school year to ensure that all seniors could attend the end of the year camping trip to Soaring Eagle Lodge. It was especially helpful for those coming from homes with limited financial means. The money raised was also used to purchase materials needed for the week spent on the mountain.

Upon arrival at camp, as a special keepsake, each student found a copy of a book, showcasing the history of Soaring Eagle Lodge, placed on the bunks in their cabins. Within the pages, adventures to be experienced while staying there were suggested. It was also a helpful resource when it came to collecting items from the forest. For example, ferns were okay to pick, but poison ivy was discouraged.

During the week, Running Deer taught them that a cold ember from the fire could be used to sketch scenes found in nature. He also showed them that red berries, clay and various plants, could be used to add color to their drawings.

After returning to school, part of their assignment would be to put together a scrapbook. Pressed leaves, wildflowers, photographs, and stories of time spent with their classmates, were possible ideas to think about when compiling their memory filled books. Disposable cameras, colored pens & pencils and a variety of scrapbooking materials were given to each student, to help with the project. Their final grade could ultimately affect their GPA, so needless to say, it was very important to pay attention and put in the effort, if they hoped to make a good grade.

The counselors encouraged each student to use their minds and their imaginations to look outside the box. The more creative they were, the higher their grade would be. There were a few students who were barely passing and with the graduation ceremony looming in the near future, the pressure was on to do well.

A beautiful sunrise... crisp mornings... delicious meals... bee stings... a rain shower... sunshine... deep blue skies... puffy white clouds... small cuts... scrapes and bruises... laughter... a few tears... a first kiss... a broken heart... an argument or two... forgiveness... a fish caught... snapshots taken... clean water... swimming in the lake... sunburns... an injured bird... a few more tears... friendship... misplaced items... things found... a stunning sunset... music... crackling logs... smoke from a campfire... roasted marshmallows... a story told... starry nights... a full moon...

Memories accumulated... made for a story worth telling...

The week flew by and Saturday morning arrived faster than anyone thought possible. It was their final full day of camp and it began as all the others had, with Thaddeus on the bagpipes. Although that first morning had started out kind of rough, the following wakeup calls had actually grown on the campers and the Scotch-Irish Rooster had found a special place in each heart. The students knew they were going to miss Mr. Barron and his antics, and he was certain to be memorialized in each and every scrapbook. Thaddeus was a flamboyant character, and many a disposable camera had captured the full scope of his colorful palette.

When chopping wood, Thaddeus dressed as a lumberjack. When playing his guitar, he was a hippie. Everyone knew what to expect when the bagpipes were playing, but when he returned to the kitchen to assist Cookie, he was dressed as a French chef. When he sat next to Running Deer at story time, he wore the garb of a mountain man, and on Italian Night… he wore a tuxedo and was playing the violin! His hair was slicked back with grease and his beard and moustache were waxed. Yes, Thaddeus Barron was genuinely humorous, a wonderful source of entertainment, and was loved by everyone.

On that final, Saturday morning, Thaddeus walked into the lodge in a pink terrycloth robe with matching pink furry slippers on his feet. Large pink rollers adorned his hair and beard… and a few small ones were tangled in his chest hairs. He wasn't much help to Cookie that morning as he was mostly kept busy posing for snapshots.

After breakfast, the students automatically headed to the amphitheater. There was a lot of chatter, as they were eager to hear what their final adventure would involve. When the last student arrived, Mr. Sherman, standing front and center, whistled to get everyone's attention. Several relevant announcements needed to be shared with the group before taking off for the summit.

"Ok, everybody… listen up! Today, will be a very long day and we need to get on the trail as soon as possible. I see that the majority were listening last night when I told you all what you'd need to bring along this morning. Thank you for being good listeners! I'm going to turn it over to Mr. Barron and he's going to tell you what will be happening today. Please, pay attention!" "Mr. Barron, the stage is yours…"

"Thank you, Mr. Sherman... and my thanks also goes out to Miss Trent and all of the hardworking counselors. You've been just terrific! I've enjoyed getting to know each and every one of you... and all of you students as well! It won't be the same when you leave tomorrow. I love you all like you were my own, and seeing as how I don't have any children of my own... I can only hope that one day you'll come back to visit me. Maybe spend a summer working here? Either way, don't be strangers."

Thaddeus pulled a red bandana from his pocket and blew his bulbous nose loudly into it. He wiped a stray tear from his eye and was touched when he heard more than a few sniffles in the crowd. To break the momentary mood of sadness, he held out his bandana to the crowd and said, "Anyone??"

Laughter erupted, as several of the young people put their hands out in front of their faces, shook their heads vigorously, and cried out, "NO, THANKS!!"

"Ok, well, if I don't have any takers, let's get down to business! Today, we will be hiking up the trail to the top of the mountain. Cookie has made a special lunch for us, and I know this because I couldn't wait to eat mine... so I already did! Right after breakfast! Cookie was none too pleased with me, but God love him, he did find it in his heart to pack me another one! Brown bag lunches are in boxes at the top of the steps and you'll each want to grab one before hitting the trail. Grab a few water bottles too! I also want to remind you to take advantage of your last civilized bathroom break. We'll be roughing it for the rest of the day... and I'll tell you how that works when the need arises!"

Groans could be heard from most of the girls, but the boys just smiled.

"We'll take breaks along the way, but it's gonna take a good three and a half hours to reach the summit. The bald eagle is a rare bird, and if we're lucky, we'll get to see one or two of them soaring on the breeze. Keep your cameras and binoculars handy at all times!"

"Also, along the way, be on the lookout for eagle feathers. They are rare treasures... and difficult to find. According to Indian Legend, they bring good luck to the person who finds one, and speaking of which, if you happen upon one today it means you get a T-bone steak tonight! The rest will get hamburgers and hot dogs."

A cheer went up into the air as eyes sparkled with the possibility of finding a cherished feather and eating a steak!

"Not only will you be fed like a king... or queen... but you'll get the honor of carving your name into Inspiration Aspen. Not far from the lodge is a special tree. It's special because it's the biggest aspen tree I've ever seen! And I've seen a lot of them in my time. Only those who reach the summit and find a gen-u-ine eagle feather, will get to leave their mark on the tree. So! Daylight's burning! Grab a lunch and some water and visit the restrooms. We'll meet at the trailhead after that!"

By 8:00 they were on their way up the mountain.

UP WE GO...

"Left... left... left, right, left!! Left... left... left, right, left!! See us hiking up the hill... ain't no cars ain't no roadkill! Are we there yet, no we're not... do we stink, oh yes... we're HOT!! Sound off..."

Wallace had taken it upon himself to lead the students in their upward march, and Daisy Wilson could take no more!

"COMPANY........ HALT!!" shouted Daisy.

Some of the dusty hikers stopped immediately in their tracks, causing a few to run into the person in front of them.

"Mr. Sherman... I beg you! You've GOT to do something with Wallace! He's shattering the peace and tranquility that some of us might like to enjoy! I, for one, would like to hear the birds chirp... the wind blow through the trees... or maybe even hear a mountain lion ROAR!" Daisy, pointing her finger in Wallace's direction, continued by saying, "Anything... but THAT!!"

Mr. Sherman turned to face the tired kids.

"I think it's time for a break. Thaddeus, what do you say?"

"I say we continue up the trail for another five minutes or so, and we'll be at Trapper's Creek. We can freshen up there, rest in the shade, drink some water, and eat a snack. From the creek, it's less than an hour to the summit, and I'm in agreement with Daisy on this last leg of the journey. Silence would be golden. If we want to actually see some wildlife in its natural habitat, we might want to think about not scaring them off. But in Wallace's defense, I would like to commend him for keeping the grizzlies away. I'm certain that if they were in the area... they no longer are!"

"Grizzlies??!" squeaked Wallace.

Mr. Sherman was grateful to have such a knowledgeable guide. Thaddeus knew his way up and down the mountain like the back of his hand, and sure enough, Trapper's Creek was right where he said it would be. They heard the welcoming sound of the water tripping and falling over rocks, shortly before seeing it. It was a welcomed sight indeed.

Upon arrival, dirty hands dove into the icy cold water, scooping it up to be splashed on hot, sweaty faces. It was oh so refreshing, and visibly invigorating.

Searching for a place to rest, flat rocks along the creek were claimed for sitting upon, as were pine trees, for leaning against. Some chose to stretch out their tired muscles on small areas of soft grass. Grass, that was also perfect for laying down on to grab a quick powernap.

Snacks of fresh fruit and trail mix were gobbled up and bottles of water were greedily consumed. Fuel in the tank made for happier hikers.

After a twenty-minute break, they clambered back onto their feet and continued to march up the mountain, where along the way, Maxwell Darington would be the first hiker to find a sacred eagle's feather.

"I like mine medium rare... thank you very much!!" smiled the dancing boy proudly waving the beautiful feather. Everyone cheered, congratulating him on his find.

The path was at times steep and uneven, but youth definitely had its advantages. Those who were not in the best physical condition were still able to make the climb, but they slowly moved to the back of the line to follow at a pace suitable for them.

Thaddeus stopped several times along the way to allow stragglers to catch up. He used the opportunity to highlight fascinating points of interest, such as the obvious thinning of the trees as they neared the summit. Trees just couldn't grow and thrive at certain elevations. A fact of nature. He also demonstrated how sound echoed and reverberated when one shouted between the mountains. Wallace was especially excited with that nugget of knowledge! Being the well-known loud mouth of the bunch, he had to try it out.

"Hellooooooo... helloooo... hellooo... hello......"

Several eyes rolled at the sound of Wallace's voice echoing all around them, and the hike continued.

As they drew closer to the top of the mountain, Miss Trent felt compelled to say, "What a beautiful day! Don't you think? Perfect weather! A lovely day for a walk in the woods! I'm just tickled to be here! Aren't you, Jacob, Daisy... everybody? Let's ALL find eagle feathers! Hey... Look up there! Isn't that an eagle up on that rock?! What a lovely bird..."

They had been blessed with sunshine and warm temperatures for the entire day and Miss Trent hadn't held back whenever she saw a clump of wildflowers, a pine cone, a rock, squirrels, etc.

After a while it became almost annoying and a few of the students began quietly imitating her as they walked along. Soon, others joined in the fun, by raving as well when they saw a bird land on a branch or a raccoon or rabbit cross the trail.

"Aren't they lovely?!" exclaimed Shayne. And when a deer suddenly appeared up ahead on the trail, Derek shouted, "Isn't he just a dear... DEER?!!"

Mr. Sherman walked up behind the boy nudging him on the shoulder. Derek turned to see his counselor shaking his head. Message received.

As they neared the top, they noticed that the air was cooler, the breeze was stronger, and the change in temperature had the power to improve the attitude of even the crabbiest hiker.

The sky was a deep blue color that was seldom seen in other parts of the world. Thaddeus pointed out an eagle's nest that was built upon a jagged rock protruding from the mountainside. With binoculars, three baby eagle's heads could be seen peeking out over the edge of the nest.

"Wow! That's amazing!" said Jake. "Do you think Wallace could shimmy over there and snag a few feathers? I don't know about the rest of you, but a steak sounds good to me!" A round of laughter bounced off the mountains.

When they finally reached the very top, a cheer went up from the crowd! Boots had rubbed blisters on several feet, but when they finally were able to experience the view from the summit, all pain was forgotten.

As they gazed out over the panoramic view, they marveled at all that surrounded them. When asked to choose one word to describe their first impression of what they were seeing, a variety of words floated on the breeze... breathtaking... magical... stunning... majestic... unbelievable... inspirational... cool!

After everyone had had their initial fill of the sights before them, Thaddeus had them take a seat on the ground. He asked them to close their eyes and observe a moment of silence. He encouraged them to let the wind wash over them... to allow it to carry all of their cares away. He asked the students to reflect back on everything that led up to this very moment in time, and then to let it all go...

As he scanned the young faces, he witnessed joy, inner peace, awe, and some internal struggles. Varying degrees of acceptance and sadness, were also evident.

When his eyes landed on the pair wearing the dark sunglasses, a shadow passed over his face and a chill ran down his spine. Derek and Shayne. One look at them told him, intuitively, that they were in mortal danger. He wasn't exactly sure how he knew this... he just knew it.

The two teenagers wore identical looks on their faces. A mirrored reflection, portraying darkness. There were really no other words for it. Concealing the vibrancy of youth, the evil shadow that hovered over them and on them, was unmistakable. Thaddeus had witnessed it before... many, many years ago... and the memory shook him to the core.

Turning his eyes away from them, he said, "Ok... you can open your eyes now."

Many of the students stood up to stretch and to retrieve items from their daypacks. With the sudden bustle of activity, Thaddeus took the opportunity to edge nearer to Shayne and Derek.

"Why don't you two take a moment to appreciate the grandeur of our surroundings with your sunglasses off. You'll find that the naked eye sees so much more... in living color. Your shades alter the experience entirely."

After scowling, Shayne reluctantly yielded to his suggestion. When she lifted off her sunglasses, Thaddeus saw the instant transformation. Where *imprisonment,* moments before had been starkly evident, *freedom,* had prompted the change in the young woman's features.

"Derek! He's right! Look how beautiful it is from up here!"

Derek stood as still as a statue made from stone. Shayne reached out and grabbed the glasses off of his face. He quickly covered his eyes with his hands, temporarily blinded by the sun. After grumbling and rubbing his eyes, his vision adjusted to the bright light.

"Wow. You're right, Shayne. This is really something!"

Thaddeus gave them a private moment to enjoy their mutual experience as they stood shoulder to shoulder staring out at the panoramic view.

"Derek… Shayne… don't forget to look at things as they really are. Behind those sunglasses you're missing out on more than you'll ever know. If you want to give them a good fling over the edge here… I won't tell anyone."

"What??! Are you kidding? No way! We like our sunglasses! A lot!! We paid good money for these babies! Why would we throw them away?!"

Derek put his back on and Shayne followed suit. Thaddeus chose to back down and walk away, but not without a troubled spirit. *LORD willing, there will be another opportunity to continue this conversation…*

"Look, everybody! An eagle's feather!!" Claire was waving her find high in the air above her head.

"Minnie SPEEEEEAKS!! Or is that… squeaks?!"

Claire's countenance fell. She lowered her eyes when Shayne's hurtful words squelched her excitement, but Daisy and Max were quick to come to Claire's defense.

Putting her arm around the crestfallen girl's shoulders, Daisy said, "That's terrific, Claire! Can I see it up close?"

"Congratulations, Claire! Some people are just jealous. That's all! Celebrate your moment, and we can eat our steaks together tonight! How do you like yours cooked?" smiled Max.

Thaddeus suddenly interrupted the group, diverting the focus from Claire and her feather to the majestic eagle flying overhead.

"Look! Up there!! Isn't she beautiful... soaring in the bright blue sky?!"

A mournful cry, carried on the wind, reached the ears of the witnesses below. Heads were twisting and turning with excitement as cameras clicked in rapid succession. The lone eagle gliding on the breeze, circled the mountaintop and then disappeared from view.

"She's more than likely heading for her nest... but what a treat! I am so glad that you were all able to see her fly!"

Derek then piped up, "What's the big deal? It's just a bird. She didn't offer up a steak dinner for me... soooo... whatever!"

Mr. Sherman just stood there, shaking his head in disappointment, whereas Thaddeus, noticing that the troubled boy was still wearing his sunglasses, nodded his head knowingly. Both men were equally concerned for Derek and his future. They were certain that they would each have more to say to him when the opportunity presented itself. Possibly, later tonight?

When things looked like they were settling down, Miss Trent advised the group to have a seat and eat their lunch. Afterwards, they were encouraged to share their past week's favorite experience with their classmates.

A few believed the best times were found during free time, others were fascinated by lessons learned from Running Deer, many agreed that the Scotch-Irish Rooster was the most memorable highlight, but several of the boys stated that it was all about the food!

Soon, it was time to wrap things up and head back down the mountain. Before leaving, they were told to scan the ground for trash. They wanted to make sure the summit was left in the same condition as when they'd arrived.

Brown bags, sandwich bags, wrappers and empty water bottles were stuffed into daypacks, and the adults went behind them, doing a quick once over. When the area was deemed acceptable, they began their trek back down off the mountain, accompanied by an all too familiar sound...

"Left... left... left, right, left! Left... left... left, right, left!! See us hiking down from here... are we there yet? Nowhere near!!! Can we LEAVE two at the top? Take a vote and..."

"WALLACE............ STOP!!!"

This time, the voice of reason belonged to Mr. Sherman.

CHOSEN

Trapper's Creek was a welcomed sight to the fatigued hikers making their way back down from the summit. Looking like wilted flowers in need of a good rain shower, they were all in desperate need of revival.

Hiking boots and soggy socks were peeled off and aching feet were happily submerged into the cool, clear water of the creek. Blisters were compared and assessed, and adhesive bandages were passed around by the counselors.

After a good soak in the healing water, bare naked feet were propped up in the sunshine. The sun's rays felt heavenly, and there were plenty of oohs and aahs to be heard amongst the lucky recipients of its warmth.

The night before the hike, the students were told to include an extra pair of socks in their daypacks. Those who had paid attention were more than happy to put on a clean, dry pair over their bandaged feet. The less attentive to instruction were forced to suck it up and put their wet, smelly socks back on... or... they had to get creative.

"Ten bucks to anyone willing to part with a fresh pair of socks!" said Jake as he held up a ten-dollar bill to tempt the crowd. When he found that he had no takers he continued, "Ok... TWENTY! But that's my final offer!"

Socks of various colors, shapes and sizes were pulled from packs and waved wildly in the air.

"SOLD!! From the young man in the back with the pair of extra-cushioned, reinforced heels and toes! God bless you, man!"

There were others in need, besides Jake, and buyers and sellers continued to barter back and forth until the supply ran out and the economy tanked.

The hikers were given a five-minute warning before the last leg of the journey was to begin. Boots were laced up, bottles of water consumed, and the group started lining up on the trail. With adults interspersed between the students, Thaddeus took the lead, setting the pace. It was a sensible plan that seemed to allow for an orderly descent.

Chatter along the way was entertaining. For the most part, they all agreed that going downhill was easier than uphill, eagle feathers were hard to find, Cookie was the best cook ever, and Miss Trent's pith helmet would indeed make a great planter for Mr. Sherman's desk!

At approximately the halfway mark, the weary hikers quieted down and became heavily lost in thought. The breeze died down as shadows deepened on the forest floor, and the repetitive motion of placing one foot after the other had a mesmerizing effect on the travelers. As they plodded along, the stillness surrounding them could be described as almost otherworldly.

Soon, they entered a section of the forest known as Mystic Woods. Running Deer had referenced it briefly when he taught them lessons pertaining to the natural habitat on the mountain.

He told them how the trail wove its way back and forth like the tail of a snake. He also shared that the canopy above was so dense in places that the heavy foliage forbade the sunlight to find its way to the forest floor. If a ray of light suddenly appeared, it should be considered a gift from the Higher Power.

As they walked along the serpentine path, Shayne was the first one to hear it. The sound of a wooden flute, seemingly floating on the breeze, had captured her attention and she stepped aside, letting those behind her pass by. Listening more closely, the soft and gentle tune made the air she breathed feel almost intoxicating.

"I've heard this before... but where...?" whispered the spellbound girl.

Shayne stepped back in line, allowing the music to pull her down the trail. Puzzled, yet intrigued, she walked along until she noticed a smaller path branching off to the left. Without a second thought, she veered off the main trail and followed the path that would take her away from the group and into the woods. Mrs. Welch had been walking directly behind Shayne, but she never noticed the girl exiting the trail.

Derek heard it next and when the mysterious music surrounded him, he thought of his mother.

Did mom sing to me when I was a baby? This sounds so familiar...

He too, saw the fork in the trail, and didn't hesitate to take it. Like Shayne, once again, no one witnessed his departure from the group.

The primitive sound from the wooden flute continued to play. Maxwell was humming along to the hypnotic music, and was following so close behind Mr. Sherman, that he almost stepped on the heel of his hiking boot. Subconsciously, he switched from humming to whistling.

When Max reached the section where the path branched off the main trail, he turned to follow it, and Jake Davis was right behind him.

Jacob never played an instrument. He did his playing on the football field under the Friday night lights, but he'd always enjoyed listening to music by cranking it up in his truck. The music he was hearing, hanging in the air amongst the trees, was different though. He wasn't sure what it was, but he knew that he had to find its source. When he saw his friend up ahead step off the trail, he naturally branched off from the class and jogged to catch up with him.

Wallace had been walking in front of Daisy when he suddenly stepped to the side and turned to grab her arm. Pulling her off the trail, he put his finger up to his lips and whispered, "Shhhhh... listen."

The two of them stared at each other, then turned and watched the rest of the students and counselors walk on without them. The hikers filed past them as if they weren't even there.

Not wishing to break the spell, Wallace whispered, "Can't they hear it too? What is it? A flute, maybe? And that song... I know it... but how do I know it??"

This time, Daisy grabbed his arm, dragging them both back onto the trail. It wasn't long before the fork in the path was revealed to them, and following the music, they were not far behind those who had gone before them.

Claire was the very last hiker in line, walking directly behind Miss Trent. Periodically, the counselor would turn around to check on her, and each time, Claire would smile and say, "All's well!"

When Claire heard the enchanting music coming from what she believed to be a wooden flute, she was instantly captivated.

The sound seemed to be floating and hanging in the air. *Amazing!*

Did my grandmother sing this song to me when I was young? What were the words? Oh my... I can't remember...

Claire stopped in her tracks and watched Miss Trent's pith helmet bob up and down, as her counselor walked on without her. Mesmerized by the motion, and by the tune playing on the breeze, the young girl just stood there staring, until the helmet disappeared around a bend in the trail.

Standing alone in the darkened forest, the bashful girl closed her eyes and let the music move around and through her.

Reaching up to the cord around her neck, she ran her thumb and index finger down it until she was able to grasp the hidden raindrop. Lifting it from beneath her pale, yellow T-shirt, she brought it to her lips and gently kissed the surface of the precious gemstone.

When she opened her eyes, she saw a ray of sunlight penetrating the canopy above, and shining down on the path up ahead. With newfound courage, she quickly returned the raindrop to its place of safety and swiftly walked to meet the light in front of her. *I can do this... I can do this... I MUST do this...*

Seven, had been chosen and called to take the path less traveled, and so... they did!

SOJOURNERS

A gentle breeze stirred the stillness, lifting the melody and carrying it through the fragrant forest. Drifting and turning, the music dipped and soared high above the treetops, moving the seven along with it. The narrow path continued leading them upward to a clearing on top of a grassy knoll. The trees surrounding the area left a window up above for the sunlight to shine through.

Shayne, Derek, Maxwell, Jacob, Daisy, and Wallace were standing together in the center of the opening when Claire arrived. As soon as she joined them, the wind picked up, the branches overhead began to swirl and dance, and the forest lullaby played on...

As the music came near, it softened, instilling a quiet sense of peace within the seven of them. Glancing around the circle, their eyes locked and shifted, moving to the beat. Communicating solely with their eyes, they acknowledged the fact that something bigger than themselves was happening here and when the lilting song from the invisible flute hushed to a mere whisper, Max spoke, breaking the spell.

"Does anyone have any idea what's going on here?"

Daisy was the next one to find her voice.

"I think we're supposed to follow the music."

"I agree, but doesn't it seem kind of odd that we were the only ones to hear it?"

"Yes, it was kinda weird, but I don't think we had a choice. Once I heard it, I had to follow it. It was out of my control, and I'm pretty sure it was the same for all of you... because here we are."

They began nodding in agreement as their eyes were drawn to a single white dove flying in a circle overhead. It landed on a nearby pine branch and cooed softly, becoming part of the same mysterious music that continued to play all around them.

Shayne turned to Wallace and said, "You're the science guy. Can you explain to us how a forest full of trees are singing to the... one, two, three, four, five, six, seven of us?"

"I wish I could. If I could, I'd market this experience! I'd make a bunch of money and buy four mansions. One for every season. I'd live large... huge... ginormously huge! I'd own race horses, have indoor and outdoor swimming pools, indoor and outdoor tennis courts, and I'd have lots of cars! A Lamborghini... a Porche`... a '67 Ford Mustang... a..."

"ENOUGH, Wallace!" Daisy held her hand up to his face.

Jacob was the next to speak.

"It's really quite simple..."

"SIMPLE? Really?! Please, Jake, do tell us how 'simple' it really is! I'm curious..." piped up Derek.

"Well... stuff happens, and then you die. THIS... would be, *the stuff*."

"Oh dear, you think we're going to die, Jacob?" cried a frightened Claire.

"I don't mean right this very minute, but someday we will! Today, we're here… wherever this may be, and I think we should just go with it. You know… not fight it."

Claire automatically reached for the raindrop hanging from her neck. The smooth feel of it in her hand, the cooing dove, and the beautiful song floating in the air, calmed her rattled spirit.

"I agree with Jake. I say we go for it! See where it leads us… but I think we need to establish a leader. I nominate Jake!" said Daisy.

"I second that!" said Max.

"Wait a minute! Why him and not me?" whined Wallace.

"Cuz you're our 'science guy,' Wally! You already have a title!" chimed in Derek.

"Ok, that's enough. It's settled. Jake is the obvious choice. He's Captain of the football team and he appears to know his… 'stuff!' Majority wins! The forest floor is yours, Jacob. What's our next move?" asked Shayne.

"Well, for starters, let's find some water. My water bottle is bone dry and I'm thirsty. I sorta forgot to fill my bottle at Trapper's Creek… kinda like when I forgot to toss in that extra pair of socks, but that was the best twenty-dollar bill I ever spent!"

"On second thought, are we SURE we want Captain America here to be our leader? I think he may have suffered one too many concussions on the field!" quipped Derek.

Putting an end to the discussion, Shayne proclaimed that it was done, and they should all just move along. Overhead, the snowy white bird lifted off from its perch and circled above them once again.

"We're supposed to follow him," announced Claire, pointing towards the dove.

"How would you know that… and don't tell me a little bird told you!" goaded Shayne.

"Actually, one did!"

She held up the silken cord from around her neck so that all could see the drop of rain dangling at the bottom of it. The raindrop appeared to be spinning on the outside, but holding still on the inside. A soft, iridescent glow surrounded it, and if that was not amazing enough in itself, upon close inspection they saw a tiny white dove flying in a circle. All eyes immediately turned skyward to observe the white bird overhead.

They followed the dove out of the clearing to a path that was hidden within the trees. As they continued their journey, the ever-present music began to mingle with the distant sound of rushing water. Smiling, they picked up the pace, eager to find the source of the tantalizing noise.

Stepping out from amongst the trees, they were stunned by what they saw. Before them, was the most spectacular waterfall they had ever seen and the sight of it literally took their breath away. Water was rapidly cascading over the face of a massive, quartz crystal rock, turning the sizeable pool beneath it aqua in color. And the bottom of the body of water was clearly made from the same crystal.

No purer water had ever been observed. Gathering at the edge of it, each and every one of them was rendered speechless. As they stood there visually drinking it all in, they were in awe of the light playing off of the crystal bottom. It sparkled like one huge diamond, and the sound of the falling water, while loud, was somehow soothing.

With eyes glued to the miracle before them, they all dropped to their knees on the soft grass surrounding the pool. The water tumbled at the base of the fall, but was as smooth as glass in the center. Their eyes were gently drawn toward the tranqulity of the still water... where a vision with a message was awaiting each one of them...

Still waters run deep, Claire, and from their very depth... in the quiet stillness... truth can be found. When truth surfaces, it must be shared, because like oxygen, it is life sustaining. Be bold... and let it be known...

No need to push against raging waters, Maxwell. No longer a boy, yet not quite a man, you will find that after the water powerfully surges, a peaceful lull embraces the former. When continuity is established, momentum presses onward, carrying with it, hope! Keep hope, alive...

Shayne, when caught up in the swiftly moving current you will be carried downstream to places unknown. While the ride appears exhilarating, the final destination is far from where you want to be. The rapids, never resting, will move you as you raise your hand high above the white water. Reach upward for the solid branch. Reach higher still and grab hold! Never let go...

Jacob, when looking past the debris floating on the surface, you see potential... purity... new life! Always present, always within reach, always worth attaining. When what lies beneath seems obscure, look deeper... and you will find what you seek after...

Dancing in the rain, find nourishment from above, Daisy. Inevitably, dark clouds will come, blocking the sun, but tears from heaven fall downward, washing away troubling doubts and fears. After the rain, look for the rainbow. Marvel at its beauty and seek after its true meaning...

Knowing that fast water is white and deep water is black, the obvious is lost. Be forewarned, Wallace. You mustn't fail to acknowledge the undertow. Beware of the strong hand that attempts to grab your heel. Kick against it! There's a mightier hand reaching down from above to lift you to solid ground. Once there, plant your feet firmly...

In the eye of the hurricane, a temporary safe haven is found. Don't overlook the fact that the storm surrounding it demands much, Derek. When it moves, you move. Constant motion is required. Unable to outrun its power and strength, you will eventually be picked up and thrown. Your inward struggle for shelter will never cease, when trapped within the eye. Trust in the wisdom given from those who see the storm clearly for what it is... and step out...

Once delivered, the spell was broken and the water in the pool began to change from aqua, to a deep emerald green.

"Whoa! What just happened?!" exclaimed Wallace.

The sudden change in the color of the water moved Claire into action. She leaned down over the pool and reached beneath the surface to retrieve something from the bottom. Lifting seven aqua colored crystals from the water, she said, "It's important to remember this moment." She handed each of them a crystal and continued by saying, "Keep them safe... and always remember."

"How did you know those were there?" asked a puzzled Shayne. "When we arrived, the bottom of the pool held no rocks, pebbles or crystals. In fact, it seemed to mirror the smooth-as-glass surface."

Claire lifted the raindrop necklace from the security of her shirt and held it up for them to see. On close inspection, in the middle of the stone, they saw her bending down and pulling crystals from the bottom of the pool.

"WHOA!" said Wallace once again.

All of a sudden, their eyes were drawn from the necklace to the waterfall. The rushing water was turning a pale shade of lavender and within seconds, the entire pool was the same color.

"WHOOOOOOA!!" cried Wallace.

Just below the surface of the water an explosion of color burst forth from the center, as thousands of multicolored fish began swimming from out of nowhere. The tiny aquatic creatures formed a pinwheel and spun wildly in a circle, spanning the pool from middle, to water's edge.

"Whoa..." exclaimed a stunned Wallace.

All at once, the fish suddenly stopped in place. In unison, they slowly unfurled from their pinwheel formation and presented an arrow, that just so happened to be pointing to the right side of the pool.

"Whoa-ho-ho-ho-HO!!" shouted Wallace.

Derek reached out and popped Wallace on the back of his head and said, "Can't you come up with something else besides, 'Whoa?!'"

Before Wallace could respond, the waterfall ceased altogether, just as if someone had suddenly turned the spigot off to a water hose. Not a single drop was spilling over the massive face of the quartz crystal rock.

WHOA!!!" cried Derek.

Wallace cut his eyes sideways and said, "Yeah, that's right!"

The seven jumped when a loud cracking sound caught their attention. The enormous stone had suddenly turned from quartz crystal, to a mottled gray boulder. The large rock was covered in patches of moss and lichen and it looked like a waterfall would normally look, when happened upon in the woods, except, no water tumbled over it.

The pool had reverted back to its normal state, looking more like a pond than anything. Brown, gray, white and golden colored rocks and pebbles lined the bottom, and the brightly colored fish were the only things remaining from the astonishing experience. The "arrow" was now pointing to a small creek heading away from the body of water, and the little fish swam quickly towards it, and into it.

"Did anyone notice that outlet before?" questioned Jake.

A resounding, "No!" filled the air.

"Come on! We're going that way!"

LISTENING

A relaxing pace was set by the colorful school of tiny fish as they meandered downstream. The group of seven settled into a collective mood of quiet reflection as they followed along beside the creek. Deep in thought, they didn't notice when the fish disappeared.

Wallace stopped, breaking the silence. "I think we should build a treehouse like that Robinson family from Switzerland did! We could tame a few deer and race them. We could live off the land and when we get tired of life in the wild, we can go back to civilization and go to Hollywood. Make a movie! Get really rich and live in a huge mansion on the beach. Have crazy-wild parties, fly to tropical islands and drink those fruity drinks with the little umbrellas. We could cut a record deal! I don't know about the rest of you... but I can sing! We could hang out with the stars, walk the red carpet and have our pictures plastered all over the tabloids. Eat caviar... drink champagne... have our own reality show. Or maybe we can be on Okra's talk show! Say... doesn't she have her own network?" Wallace looked at them with all seriousness.

"Are you nuts, Wallace?! Because the odds are greater that we'll be attacked and eaten by grizzly bears, long before you can even pick out a tree for your house!" Max just shook his head at Wallace, in disbelief.

"Did you say grizzly bears?! I forgot about them!!" said a visibly shaken Wallace.

"Wallace Robinson... hmmm... it has a nice ring to it! I say we leave the deer racer to his adventure, and the rest of us travel on out of here!" said Derek.

Jake took control of the conversation by saying, "Let's just keep following the fish. I'm thinking they know the way out of here."

All eyes were diverted towards the creek, only to find that their tiny guides were gone.

"Hey... wait a minute! Where'd they go??! Now that's just great! Fantastic! What are we supposed to do now?! Thanks for distracting us, Wally! This is your fault!" quipped a frustrated Shayne.

"Wait! Listen! Do you hear that?" Daisy was the first to hear the music, but this time it didn't sound like it was coming from a wooden flute. It sounded more like a windchime, singing in the wind. "It's the same tune..."

They stood still, listening for a moment. The music was growing noticeably stronger and louder, as it was brought to them on the breeze.

"It's so beautiful..." Claire pushed her way through the group and began walking away from the water, deeper into the forest.

"Should we bother asking her if she knows the way?" said Max.

"Nope! I think we've already established that she's got the hotline to higher thinking. It'd be best to just follow her..." replied Daisy.

Trailing after the quiet girl of the bunch, they journeyed further and further into the thickening woods. As they traveled in, the canopy above became noticeably dense, shutting out what little sunlight was left. When Derek pointed out the lack of light, they were all pretty amazed that their eyes had adjusted, and that they were still able to see where they were going.

They squeezed through heavy brush and climbed over fallen trees, and as they moved along, Shayne noticed that the trees seemed to be getting bigger and bigger.

"Ok, I'm feeling a bit like Alice in Wonderland here! Either these trees are getting bigger and bigger or I'm getting smaller and smaller... and if ANY of you see that freaky cat with the big wide grin... let me know... cuz he really creeps me out!" shuddered Shayne.

"I think we'll see a mountain lion first," said Derek.

"Oh, GREAT! Grizzlies AND mountain lions?!!" cried Wallace.

"And don't forget Sasquatch, Wally! I'm pretty sure he lives in these parts and uses these trees for toothpicks!" said Derek with a wicked grin.

"Look!!" cried Daisy, pointing straight ahead.

Wallace covered his eyes with both hands and whimpered, "Please don't make me... please don't make me... please don't make me..."

"No, look! It's Tinker Bell!" she cried, while popping him on the arm.

Wallace opened his eyes and heaved a heavy sigh. "Ok, enough of the fairy tales. There's a reasonable explanation for your Tinker Bell. She is in fact a mere firefly. Actually, a quite large firefly... but none the less, just a firefly. Mystery solved."

"Come on guys! Let's follow the blinking fly! She looks like she knows where she's going!" commanded Jake.

The flickering light zipped back and forth between the trees and the seven followed after it. Tripping and stumbling, they were led uphill and downhill, and past a rather large clump of pine trees. They were huffing and puffing when the woods abruptly ended, delivering them into an open meadow that was flooded with blinding sunlight.

"Dang, that's bright! Yikes!! Where are my sunglasses?!"

"They're on your head, dummy!"

"No, they're not, wise guy!"

"They're hanging on your shirt, nimrod!!"

"Mine are in my pack!"

"I think I dropped mine!"

"Don't step on them... no, wait a minute, here they are!"

As they clamored after their shades, Claire just shook her head. She was the only one at the Flower Festival who didn't buy sunglasses, and she was grateful. She was convinced that they were evil! She agreed that the sunshine was blinding, but she was willing to tough it out. Or maybe not. Reaching for the raindrop, when her hand came in contact with the comforting stone, the light seemed a lot less blinding.

Tinker Bell was gone, but the music played on with the tinkling chime-like tune continuing to swirl all around them. To Claire, it sounded melodic and beautiful, but to the other six it seemed almost agitating. Their stony expressions were at times disrupted by a sneer or a smirk, clearly emphasizing their displeasure. She just wished they would take those ugly glasses off and lighten up!

The mood changed significantly when they were distracted by the meadow's transformation. Delicate yellow wildflowers began sprouting up before their eyes, forming a golden path across the grassy field.

"Follow the yellow brick road... or is that... the yellow flowered path?! One thing's for sure... I'm not skipping or singing my way down it, and if monkeys start flying overhead, I say we catch them, wring their scrawny necks and eat them! I'm hungry!" spouted Shayne.

The others never responded to Shayne's remark, they just kept their eyes forward and started walking on the floral pathway. The blossoms, being crushed beneath their boots, added a lovely fragrance to the trek, but Claire was the only one to notice it. She also noticed, upon glancing back, that the flowers seemed to be evaporating into thin air behind them. It was looking more and more like their only option was to keep moving forward.

Claire wanted to say something, but she stopped herself. Being timid and shy definitely had its drawbacks. She was pretty sure that they wouldn't listen to anything she had to say anyway, while wearing those evil shades, so she just kept her thoughts and ideas to herself... and the group journeyed onward.

The bright yellow flowers led them across the meadow and through a glen, eventually bringing them to a grove of aspens. The trees were tall and elegant with soft green leaves dancing in the gentle breeze. The branches swayed back and forth and seemed to be waving the seven into their presence.

"Take off your glasses so you can see how truly beautiful these aspens are. You really can't appreciate them through those tinted lenses..." encouraged Claire.

As they entered the grove, one by one they lifted their sunglasses, placing them on their heads.

"Wow! They really are something special! I wonder if the wood from these trees would make a good boat? You know, or maybe you don't know... but my dream is to build a boat one day and sail away," said Max.

"I think this wood would look better in a firepit or maybe it would make decent furniture for Wally Robinson's tree house! You know, it's not too late to leave him here..." stated Derek.

"Be quiet and listen!!" said Jacob.

The seven travelers stood silently, shoulder to shoulder, trying to hear what Jake was hearing. They noticed that the same melody was still floating in the air, but it also sounded like the leaves above them were either singing or whispering. Or both?

As they walked beneath the dancing limbs, they were drawn deeper into the grove of expressive trees. Nearing the center, they were amazed to see sunlight shining down brightly upon seven flat rocks. Like dominoes falling one after the other, they proceeded to sit down on them. Once everyone was seated comfortably, a cool mist descended upon them, capturing their attention and calming their inner thoughts.

This time it was the wind, not water, that brought a special vision and message to each of them...

If left wandering in the valley with the mountain looming large, look up, Jacob. When the sun hides its face and the wind pushes against you, hold fast. Climb onward and upward until you reach the peak. The reward is mighty, and worth claiming...

Shayne... when the winter wind blows, and ice-cold fingers reach out to capture you, don't be afraid. Stand firm! The warm breath of spring will arrive to free you from your frozen captivity. Welcome the change...

Know that when the wind changes direction, Claire, it does so with purpose. Although you cannot see it, when it nudges you, let it carry you upward. Embrace its power, by acknowledging its guidance...

Wallace, the difference between a whisper and a shout seems great when carried by the wind... but which is greater? Know that when fear is conquered, that which was spoken loudly will be answered with a quiet response...

Dare to run swiftly as you hold on to the string that anchors the kite. Watch it soar! Stand still... Derek... and see the wind lift it high above the clouds. Fly with it... and it will carry you beyond your wildest dreams...

The ride is sweet when prevailing winds fill your billowing sails to full capacity. With the lighthouse in view, your ship will glide effortlessly through deep waters. Enjoy the freedom that comes with it, Maxwell... it is a gift...

Daisy... like the sparrow, when caught in an updraft, you will be wise to lean into the wind. As you continue upward, aim for the clouds... so that the path below can be revealed to you. Put one foot in front of the other... and press on...

The mist began to slowly dissipate, once the messages were delivered, and the seven remained quiet and reflective as they absorbed all that had been shared with them.

Jacob was the first one to speak. Pointing up towards the leaves in the trees, he questioned, "Is it just me, or have those leaves changed color?"

Sunlight, filtering through the foliage, made it difficult to look up, so the six young people with sunglasses perched on their heads dropped them down over their eyes. When they looked back up, the leaves had turned from dark green, to red, to orange, and then gold.

The light breeze that had been present, suddenly ceased, and seven aspen leaves fell to the ground at Claire's feet. The moment they touched the ground they turned to solid gold. Claire leaned over and gathered them up.

"To remember…" she stated simply, as she handed them out.

Just as suddenly as the leaves up above had changed color, they began to wither and turn brown. Next, the wind picked up considerably and the dried-up leaves rained down on the travelers.

"Looks like it's time to move on!" shouted Jake, over the sound of the wind.

When it began to howl and the temperature dropped dramatically, dark clouds released pelting rain that immediately turned into heavy snowflakes.

"Follow me!!" hollered Jake.

He led them out of the trees and back into the meadow. The grass was almost completely covered in snow by then, and they had to battle the wind while trudging through it.

The six, still wearing sunglasses, seemed unfazed by the cold. They steadily marched behind their leader while Claire brought up the rear. The snow was now blowing sideways, and shaking uncontrollably, the frozen girl could barely keep up with them.

Just when Claire thought she would fall over and freeze to death, Jake led them to an opening in the side of the mountain. Those immune to the frigid temperatures walked calmly into the cave's entrance. Claire, on the other hand, stumbled in, crying, "Aren't you all freeeezing… like meeee??!

"NOPE! Not us. Just you, Minnie! We love the cold wind in our faces! It's invigorating! You're just not made of the right stuff, mouse girl!" taunted Shayne.

"She's right!" snapped a red nosed Wallace.

As the others nodded their heads in agreement, Shayne took the lead. She told them all to "quit their yapping," so they could "explore this hole in the mountainside and see what it had to offer!"

Claire, still shaking, wondered if they were ever going to take their glasses off. After all, they were about to plunge deeply into a cave! And who in their right mind wears sunglasses underground? She reached for the raindrop necklace and was beyond grateful when her frigid skin turned quickly from icy cold to warm and pink. This was proving to be one adventure that she would not soon forget.

THE CHAMBER

They could still hear the wind howling outside, although it was somewhat muffled due to the thick walls of the cave. Claire was absolutely grateful to be out of the freezing blizzard, but she had a bad feeling about this next leg of their journey. There was enough room in the entrance for them to huddle in a tight group, but as they moved deeper into the body of the cavern, the walls and ceiling seemed to widen out and lift up.

Jake picked up a rock and threw it as hard as he could into the darkness. They were all listening closely to hear if the projectile might hit something, indicating the depth of the thing, and when it did finally strike something solid, the sound was barely audible.

"Ok, so obviously this cave goes somewhere, and I think we should see where it takes us."

"I think that is a very, very bad idea..." shivered Claire.

"Let me guess, Mouse Girl. Your little necklace there said, 'don't doooooo it!'" mocked Shayne from behind her sunglasses.

"If you'd just take off your glasses, you'd see that it's a very bad idea," stated Claire.

Shayne lifted up her shades, looked around, and dropped them back down into place. "No thanks! I can see better with them on. Even in the dark!"

The other sunglass wearers followed suit to see if Shayne was correct, and ultimately, they agreed that their vision was better with them on.

Wallace slipped his arm out of his pack and swung it around in front of him. Unzipping the outer pouch, he retrieved a small flashlight and flipped it on.

"Boo-yah!! Follow me, soldiers!"

"Very... very bad idea..." whispered Claire, as she watched them march behind Wallace and his tiny beacon of light. She knew it was against her better judgement to follow them, but she was more afraid of being left behind. Slowly, she straggled after them.

The stony path within the interior of the mountain was noticeably slanting downward. It gently meandered with a few twists and turns, while continuing to descend deeper and deeper into the earth. Every now and then someone would temporarily lose their footing and tiny rocks would go rolling down the path. With only one flashlight, they had to walk close on the heels of the person in front of them, if they hoped to see anything at all.

"Hey! Watch it!" snapped Derek. "You almost pulled my boot off, dipstick!"

Max snapped back, "Then walk faster, speed racer!"

Without warning, Wallace's flashlight flipped off. He tried to turn it back on, but all they could hear in the dark was... click, click, click... followed by heavy breathing.

"Ok, don't panic..." said Jacob.

"Don't panic?! Don't panic?!! It's darker than Hades in here, and I don't know if you noticed or not, but there's no music in here either! Just silence. Total... black, cold silence. What are we supposed to do now?!" cried a shaken Wallace.

Suddenly, a bright white light could be seen moving towards them. Wallace heaved a sigh of relief.

"She's back! It's Tinker Bell!!" exclaimed Daisy.

A cheer went up, "Hooray for Tink!!"

The friendly firefly blinked and flashed as it led them deeper and deeper into the mountain.

"I don't like this one bit," squeaked Claire. She was convinced that they had entered the bowels of the earth, and was certain that their journey was destined to end badly.

"You don't have to like it, Minnie! You just have to keep your mousetrap shut and follow along like a good little rodent! No one wants to hear a squeak out of you!" said the mean-spirited Shayne Darby.

As soon as the last word spewed forth from her lips, the ground beneath their feet began to tremble and vibrate.

"Uh-oh! What does this mean?!"

All conversation ended when chaos erupted. The hard packed soil underfoot turned to a loose mixture of sand and pebbles, and the path fell away from beneath their feet. They immediately landed flat on their backsides and began sliding down a slippery slope. As they grappled for *anything* to hold onto, a large stream of water shot out from an opening in the left side of the cave wall, creating a waterslide underneath them. In complete darkness, screaming all the way, they careened wildly down the twisting, turning chute. When they finally reached the end of it, they were propelled straight out into midair, only to drop twenty feet down into complete darkness. Waiting to embrace them below, was a cold, dark, oily, black, bottomless body of water. The vile liquid shot up their noses and terror clutched at their throats, when they plunged feet first into the frigid murky water.

Kicking madly, the seven popped up above the surface like bobbers on a lake. Struggling to fill their lungs with oxygen, they hacked and coughed, trying desperately to rid their air passages of the nasty water.

"What the hell was that?!!!" screamed Wallace.

Daisy, panting wildly and fighting for air, cried back... "You... just said it! We're... in ... HELL!!"

Tinker Bell was no longer with them, and the darkness seemed even more oppressive than ever.

Out of fear, they moved closer together, while frantically kicking to stay above the surface. Suddenly, a whooshing sound from up above, caused them to turn their eyes upward. Far above their heads, a ring of fire mysteriously leapt to life, dimly illuminating the frightening predicament they had fallen into. Immediately, they began searching for a way out of the black pool.

It didn't take long to realize that they were encased in what appeared to be a cylindrical chamber. Resembling a silo formed from solid rock, the thought of exiting it seemed impossible, until Jake noticed a long wide ledge jutting out from the wall.

"Come on, everybody! Swim for the ledge!" he ordered.

They gladly followed his lead and began kicking their way to safety, but before they could reach the rock shelf, millions of tiny bubbles began surfacing from below.

"GET OUT... NOW!!!!" screamed Jacob.

The boys were stronger, and were the first ones to hurl their bodies up onto the ledge. The girls, lacking upper body strength, and numb from the cold, had to be pulled to safety, one by one. When all of them were out of harms way, they heaved a collective sigh of relief.

"THAT... WAS...INSANE!! And those bubbles aren't looking all that friendly either!!!" yelped Shayne.

All eyes were laser focused on the dark, bubbling brew as the water began to undulate, bringing hundreds of black hissing snakes to the inky surface. The venomous reptiles frantically slipped and slithered around each other, twisting and turning into an angry knot.

The dripping wet survivors stood up and plastered their bodies against the cold rock wall, distancing themselves as much as possible from the sinister mass. Fear was proving to be paralyzing, after realizing that their fate could have been much different... if not for the rock ledge beneath them.

When the cold soggy young people were confident that the snakes couldn't reach them, relief washed over each one of them, but it was short-lived when the menacing serpents began opening their fiery-red mouths. Revealing sharp silver fangs, the firelight from above only emphasized the danger the roiling mass presented. The evil informants were there to deliver seven messages to the trembling teenagers... and this is what they conveyed...

In the dark of night... Derek... there is little shelter from prying eyes! You know what you want! When you see it, take it!! On your turf, there are no rules... because you make them!

Shayne... you dig your toes into the starting block before the race begins. Leap ahead of the rest before the gun goes off! If others try to enter your lane, a well-place elbow is what they deserve! YOU... belong at the front of the pack... always!

The early bird gets the worm... Maxy... but the worm dies. Snap your fingers and watch them emerge from the dirt under your feet. Take what you want and stomp on the rest! You are in charge!

Weeds. They are nothing but weeds! Weeds can be pulled up and tossed aside... or gasoline and a match will take care of them! The end results are the same... and it's your call, Jacob!

Wally, my boy! Some say toe-may-toe... some say toe-mot-toe. You say poe-tay-toe... I say poe-tah-toe! Yada yada... the debate goes on. You're smarter than that! Stick to the facts, buddy boy, and don't let anyone tell you anything different! Ever!!

Precious flower... little Daisy. So happy. So carefree. Grown in rich soil.... blah, blah, blah! She loves me... she loves me not. What?! She loves me... she loves me... YES... she LOVES me! She just doesn't quite know it yet...

Timid little mouse... are you hungry? Would you like a piece of delicious cheese? No?? Well... an earthquake will shake things up, fair Claire, but who will catch you when you fall, tiny mouse? Me... perhaps?!! Perhaps...

After the final taunting word was hissed forth... the water exploded, and a billowing cloud of black smoke filled the chamber. The seven pulled their wet shirts up over their mouths and noses, and squeezed their eyes shut against the stinging smoke. When the acrid air began to clear, they opened their eyes and saw that the once infested water was now smooth, and snake free. With no time to waste, they began assessing their surroundings.

"Hey, look over there! It's a rope ladder!!" pointed Max.

They quickly made their way to the base of what appeared to be the most likely way out.

"Ok, Derek goes first, then Daisy, Wallace, Shayne and Max. Claire can go after that and I'll bring up the rear!" commanded Jacob.

Without argument, Derek was happy to get it started. He grabbed a rung and put one foot after the other as he climbed up the ladder. When it appeared to be safe, Daisy went next and the rest followed. When they came closer to the ring of fire, they noticed that there was a break in the illuminated circle, allowing the ladder to continue upward without burning.

"Does this ladder ever end?" whimpered an exhausted Daisy.

"It has to! Keep climbing and don't look down! Think about something else. Maybe those flowers your mother grows..." replied Derek.

When they moved further up past the firelight, once again, it began to grow dark. They continued to climb. When worry started to chip away at their resolve, help arrived just in the nick of time.

"TINK!! God bless you!" shouted an elated Daisy.

The firefly circled around them, then spiraled upward, lighting the way, as the hanging apparatus creaked and groaned under the weight of the climbers. Not long after that, the ladder brought them to another rock ledge, jutting out from the wall.

"What's with these rock shelves?! Give me solid ground and fresh air! Please!!" said an exasperated Shayne.

Tinker Bell hovered above at the top of the chamber, and the bright white light that emanated from her only emphasized the foreboding darkness of the abyss below. Only a few were brave enough to look down and the fear that it evoked in them was temporarily paralyzing.

Derek noticed that his sunglasses were gone. He looked around at his companions and noticed that they too, had lost theirs along the way. He also noticed that Claire still had the blue cord around her neck, and that puzzled him.

Once again, Tink's light was extinguished, and the seven weary sojourners were plunged into utter darkness. They reached out for each other and slammed themselves against the rock wall. The cloak of dread was heavy, and the silence was deafening. As they stood clinging to one another, thinking, *what's next*, a clear, steady voice, powerfully shattered the stillness... and the following words were released...

Standing on the edge of never, shaken by the night, I am here but you can't see me in this place that has no light.

Gripping blindness, sea of many, you are pulled out with the tide... but cling tightly to the rock and see the heavens open wide!

Flies the arrow, sweet precision, plunging ever towards the mark, it's the brightest ray of always, slicing swiftly through the dark.

Standing on the edge of never, shaken by the black of night, I am here but you can't see me in this place that has no light.

Standing on the edge of never... shaken... without sight... I am here, but you can't see me... for the blackness of the night...

A shaft of light shot forth, shining brightly down upon them. When it did, Claire ran her hand across the wall beside her and seven black onyx stones fell off into her palm. She handed one to each of her friends and simply said, "Never forget!"

The cold stones felt like burning ice in their bare hands, so they quickly shoved them into their pockets. Rubbing their palms together, they tried to warm up their hands. As they were doing this, a single, bright red fiery ember floated upwards from below, disappearing into the wall, six feet away from them.

"Follow that ember!!" shouted Claire.

Who knew Claire could shout? thought Wallace, as they all clamored after her.

The airborne chunk of wood revealed a sizeable opening in the rock wall, which then led them into a short tunnel. The glowing ember continued to float before them, eventually exiting the cave into the fresh mountain air. The tired teens raced out behind it, collapsing on the ground. With the earthen tomb in their rear-view mirror, they were grateful to be breathing clean air beneath the wide-open sky.

When first entering the cave, the weather had been winter-like, but when they exited it, mysteriously, the temperature felt more like summertime. That alone would have been something to contemplate, but as they stopped and stared at the multitude of sparks spiraling upwards into the darkening sky, they realized that now was not the time for reflection.

Far away, as a distant drum was finding its rhythm, the exhausted teenagers watched the ember that had led them to freedom, ignite a nearby pine tree...

ON SOLID GROUND

"Ruuuuuuunnnn!!!!!" screamed the seven in unison.

It was only too obvious that the wildfire was spreading rapidly, being fed by brittle twigs, dead timber and dry underbrush. As the flames leapt up the sides of tall pine trees, the fire continued to roar to life. The smell of burning wood, thick black smoke, and fear, assailed the nostrils of all within its grasp.

The terrified teenagers took off running as if their lives depended on it, which in fact, theirs did! Tearing through the trees, they tripped and fell, then jumped up and ran some more. Low hanging branches scraped their faces and arms, but they hardly noticed it as the sheer horror of the situation pressed them onward. When they thought they could run no further, they dug deep by tapping into that God given well of youthful energy, and they kept on running.

As the inferno grew, animals in all shapes and sizes seemingly appeared from out of nowhere, running beside them and around them. Every living, breathing thing had only one thought in mind. Self-preservation!

The will to survive was second nature, and determination was fiercely exhibited in the eyes of the seven young people. During the exodus, the boys kept their eyes on the girls, physically hauling them up off the ground when they fell, and dragging them along when necessary.

Jacob was thinking that if they didn't reach safety soon, the fire would overtake and consume them... and that was an extremely terrifying thought! His eyes were constantly scanning the landscape, searching for an escape from the nightmarish flight. When it finally presented itself, overwhelming relief washed over him.

The forest of trees ended abruptly and the exhausted runners tumbled out into a small grassy meadow. On the other end of it, they saw willow bushes stretching for as far as the eye could see. It looked as though a thick fog was beginning to descend upon the wispy willows, and as they drew closer to them, they could feel the welcoming moisture. It greeted them like a cool rain shower after a long stretch of hot dry weather, and they did not hesitate to run into the mist.

In the distance, the sound of the beating drum was becoming more pronounced, but the group of seven didn't give it much thought. Once inside the willows, they all stopped briefly to catch their breath. Claire reached for the blue cord around her neck. She hoped that the raindrop would give them direction in navigating their way through the fog encased maze of willows.

"It's not going to be easy... finding our way... but we must go through them... to reach the other side..." panted the out of breath girl.

We survived the hellacious cave, and an out-of-control wildfire, only to be told by too-shy Claire that a bunch of bushes are going to be a challenge? Piece of cake... thought Wallace, as he disappeared into the maze.

"Wait a second, Wallace!"

"Too late!" cried Derek, as he dashed in after him.

Without a second thought, Shayne, Daisy and Max followed suit, running in after them. Leaving Jake and Claire still standing there, the two turned towards one another.

"Sorry, Claire, but we can't just wait around and let that fire find us again! I'm going in too! Follow me!" Jake disappeared into the thick, hazy blanket of fog.

Claire looked up and saw the full moon peeking down on her through an open window in the murky sky. She shook her head and wanted to cry, but she held tightly to her raindrop necklace, knowing that with it, her courage would be restored. Entering the willows, she headed in the same general direction as her classmates.

The greenery was at least ten feet tall, and the only way to get through it all was to weave in and around the bushes, like yarn on a loom. Each one of them were fairly confident that they could find their way out, but it wasn't long before all seven were separated from one another. Ten minutes in, they were finding it difficult knowing, if they were going in circles or heading back to where they had started. Twenty minutes after that, the ground beneath their feet turned from being solid, to that of a marshy bog.

"Oh, great!" cried Shayne, "I feel like I'm walking on a waterbed! What if it springs a leak? That's right... I'll just sink to the bottom like a rock. Assuming there IS a bottom! There probably isn't one! So... it'll be... glug... glug... glug. Lights out!"

Wallace was having a similar experience as Shayne. He could have sworn that he heard a voice saying, *"Come this way,"* but when he followed it, the swampy turf became even more unstable.

The other four, battling the same fear and conditions, struggled along as best they could across the soggy moss-covered ground. Forced to backtrack, frustration set in when they felt like they were going nowhere. They occasionally hollered out after one another, but to no avail. If they heard a response it sounded too far away to consider. They realized quickly that they were on their own.

Claire, on the other hand, was having a far different experience traversing the maze. A small brown sparrow, floating on the breeze, appeared immediately after entering, and she followed the little feathered creature safely through to the other side. When she came out of the willows she was welcomed by a field of clover. Beneath the full moon, she walked out into the middle of it and laid down. Within minutes, she was fast asleep... lulled by the rhythmic drumbeat in the distance, and comforted by the sweet-smelling clover.

The six held captive by their own poor judgement and impulsive nature, wandered around in confusion for several hours. Tormented by doubts and thoughts of failure, they muddled their way through, eventually ending up in the same field as the sleeping girl.

When they found Claire fast asleep in the clover, Shayne threw both hands in the air, and cried, "THAT figures! Tell me AGAIN why we didn't all chain ourselves to Minnie Mouse?!"

Claire sat up abruptly, yawning and rubbing her eyes.

"Oh! There you are! Did you all follow that sweet little bird too?"

Before a wild-eyed Wallace could do something that he'd regret, Jacob grabbed him by the arm and replied, "Yeah... it was something like that, Claire."

"Well... that's good. I think I fell asleep. This clover smells so sweet and lovely... and it's very soft to lay on... and wait! I have a memento for each of you!"

Claire produced seven tiny birds carved from thick willow branches.

"A very sweet little bird gave these to me," she smiled, as she held out her hands.

"Well... isn't that just super, Claire, but there's no time for resting... LOOK!" Max pointed suddenly to a scene transpiring off in the distance.

On a hilltop beneath the moonlight, two figures sat across from each other at a campfire. It was impossible to tell who they were from that distance, but curiosity and the thought of warming themselves up by a *controlled* fire, urged them on.

"Come on, let's go! Maybe they can tell us where we are..." encouraged Max.

The drumbeat grew stronger and louder, the closer they came, to the pair sitting on the hill...

THE CHOICE

Spoken words were unnecessary for the two men sitting in restrained opposition, staring at one another from across the fire. As flames and smoke curled and twisted, spiraling up into the night sky, dark mahogany eyes never wavered from the steely gray pair. The age-old battle between the two opponents was destined to continue, until he who had already been defeated, accepted his fate. Until then, the silent war would rage on.

The crackling fire sent an array of sparks racing up towards the heavens. Bouncing to the rhythm of the drum, the tiny specks of light danced in the cool night air, while the two opposing warriors continued their silent conversation. Confidence, shining brightly in one, observed fear being masked in the other. Both men knew exactly where they stood.

The group of seven, walking across the field of clover, were happy to have the full moon up above to light their way through the dark.

"Look! Fireflies! Hundreds and thousands of fireflies!!" cried Daisy.

Claire, following along at the back of the pack, retrieved the necklace from under her shirt and lifted it up in front of her face. When she saw the swarm of tiny bright lights flying within the raindrop, she smiled, and returned it to its safe place.

"Wow! Pretty cool, if I do say so myself, but I wouldn't get too close to them if I were you, Shayne. That clump of tangled hair on your head looks like a good place for our little friends here to build a nest!" exclaimed Wallace.

Shayne quickly dug into her pocket for a hair band. Running her fingers through the untamed mane, she pulled her hair away from her face, twisted it around, and secured it at the nape of her neck.

Derek just stared at her in disbelief. Looking right back at him she replied, "What? Do you think nerd boy is just yanking my chain? Well... maybe he is and maybe he isn't! After the stroll through the bog, I'm not taking any chances! We should have listened to Minnie. So... moving on! I'm just going to follow the little neon bugs and avoid personal disaster, if you don't mind!" With that, she turned on her heel and marched off in the direction of the blinking fireflies.

"I guess she told you!" smirked Wallace.

In response to the jab, Derek, passing by him, slammed his shoulder into Wallace's back.

"Come on guys, knock that off... and let's get a move on! It's starting to feel a bit chilly out here and that campfire's looking mighty good about now!" said Jacob.

The sweet smell of clover, crushed beneath their boots, along with the playful display of lights, escorting them to their destination, made the hike through the field to the hill, enjoyable. With the moonlight shining down, they all agreed that this last leg of the journey would definitely be worth writing home about.

When they reached the base of the hill, they paused, looking back over the distance they'd traveled.

The field of clover... the bog in the willows... the forest, still glowing in the night sky from the raging wildfire. It was all very overwhelming to think about, but before all of that had transpired, the memory of their time spent in the dark underground sent a collective shiver up their spines.

"We could have died in that fire. We could have been sucked into the bog and never seen again... and I think we'd all rather not talk about the snakes!" said Daisy.

"I don't know. I think I might want to get a pet snake when I get back home. I could name him... Alphonse!" stated Wallace.

"You are one sick puppy, Wally. That's all I have to say about that!" replied Max.

"Why get just one? Get several of them and let them slither all over your room! I think rattlesnakes would make good pets for you, nerd boy. The rattling sound could lull you to sleep at night and I'll even help you name the rest of them. After 'A' for Alphonse, I'm thinking Beauregard, for 'B!' We could call it a science project and utilize the entire alphabet," quipped Derek.

"Alright, that's enough snake talk. Onward and upward!" said Jacob, pointing towards the top of the hill. Daisy, feeling grateful for the change in subject, shivered again as she stood beside him.

Jake and Max were the first ones to reach the top of the rise, followed by Shayne and Derek, then Claire, Daisy and Wallace. The sound of the beating drum was almost deafening, the closer they came to the men by the fire, and when they realized who the two were, the startled companions stopped dead in their tracks.

"Hey, it's the two guys from the festival..." whispered Daisy to Claire.

The Rain Mender

Just then, the swarm of fireflies that had been accompanying them, began flying in a circle around the kids and the two men. As the drumbeat quieted down, the little blinking creatures formed a bright ball of light overhead, mirroring the full moon. All eyes became riveted on the phenomenon above them, and when the glowing sphere of insects suddenly exploded like a huge sparkler on the 4th of July, the seven teens felt a sudden jolt run through them. The fireflies were gone, the two guys hadn't moved, and the tired hikers couldn't help but wonder… *what's next?*

Stryker was the first to break the silence. With a long sweep of his hand, he motioned them to the empty logs around the campfire, and said, "Have a seat, gang."

No one moved and no one said a word, until Michael turned towards them and said, "Please, make yourselves comfortable."

After a slight hesitation, they stepped over the logs and sat down, but once again, jumped… when Stryker snapped open the black briefcase that had been resting on the ground between his feet. As he lifted the lid of the shiny hinged box, he looked up at them and smirked, "A bit jumpy, are we?"

Returning his gaze to the contents within, he pulled seven pairs of sunglasses from the case. After closing it, he used the top of it to display his merchandise.

"Just shades, my friends." He presented the collection to the group as he continued, "I can see that you've all misplaced your original sunglasses, and I'd like to offer you another pair."

Locking eyes across the fire at Michael, the man in black added, "Free of charge!"

When Stryker diverted his gaze back towards the kids, his facial features softened, and with the dark shades in his hands, he stood up and circled around the back side of the teenagers.

Derek quickly swiveled on his log and held out his hand. "Thanks, I'll take a pair. They're really cool sunshades!"

With steely gray eyes shimmering in the firelight, he smiled and moved on to Shayne.

"Hey, pretty lady... we meet again. Would you care for a pair?"

Although she hesitated for a brief moment, she stretched out her hand and accepted the sunglasses, echoing Derek's sentiment.

Next, Stryker approached Daisy. The adamant girl waved both hands in front of her face, warding him off.

"I don't think so, but thanks anyway," she swiftly stated.

"I'll just set them here beside you... in case you change your mind."

Wallace, sitting right next to Daisy, without turning around in his seat, immediately lifted his hand over his shoulder and held his palm open.

"Lay em on me! I'm game!"

Stryker dropped the pair into his open hand and replied, "That's my boy! Wear them in good health!"

Claire sat bolt upright on the log next to Wallace. As the man in black drew near, her body language spoke volumes. Scooting as close to the fire as possible, she kept her back turned towards him.

"I'll just set these right here..." he whispered softly in her ear.

Max & Jake sat shoulder to shoulder. "None for me!" stated Max. "I'm good too!" added Jacob. "Thanks anyway!" they said in unison.

"Oh, come on fellas. You know you can use a good pair of sunglasses. Don't be shy..."

Stryker opened a pair and placed them on the top of Jacob's head. He advanced towards Max to do the same, but the boy jumped up and immediately threw his pair into the fire. When the glasses hit the hot fiery flames, a demonic scream pierced the night.

Claire jumped up and followed suit by kicking the pair on the log next to her in after them. A horrifying shriek ripped through the night, triggering Claire to quickly cover her ears with her hands, while tightly squeezing her eyes shut.

Stryker jumped over the log and reached into the fire with his bare hands. He pulled both pairs of sunglasses out from the flames, and the screaming immediately ceased.

"See there... not a problem!" He lifted up his hands holding the glasses, revealing that both were unscathed by the incident.

"We all have choices!" he said, as a dark shadow passed over his features. "No problem at all..."

He returned to his seat by the fire and placed the sunglasses back in the case. Those who refused his *free gift,* jumped when the lid snapped shut, while those wearing shades in the dark of the night, sported stone-cold smiles on their faces.

Next, it was Michael's turn to stand up and address the group. Walking over to Max, he put himself between the boy and the fire. Lifting the leather cord up over his own head, Michael held the raindrop out and offered it to Max.

"I believe you're ready for this now..." said Michael, and the boy confidently replied, "Yes sir, I most certainly am... and thank you!"

Michael moved over to stand in front of Shayne. He held out his hand as she lifted the sunglasses off of her face. Placing them in his open palm, she quietly thanked him for taking them. When he closed his fingers around the glasses, the evil shades turned to ash, and were immediately swept away by a sudden gust of wind.

Michael looked deeply into Shayne's troubled, ice blue eyes, and observed a solitary tear escaping from one corner. It slipped silently down her cheek, just as he was reaching into his shirt pocket. Pulling out a long sky-blue cord with raindrop attached, he offered it to the girl. She nodded and he placed it over her head.

Daisy looked at the sunglasses sitting next to her and was not quite ready to hand them over. She had left her necklace in her duffle bag back at the cabin, and had said as much when Michael approached her. He placed his hand on her shoulder, looked deeply into her eyes and said, "You'll know when the time is right to choose."

Next, he approached Jacob. Jake had decided to keep the sunglasses that were resting on the top of his head. When Michael looked deeply into his eyes, the boy said, "My raindrop necklace is hanging from the rearview mirror in my truck back home. I haven't lost it."

Michael gently smiled and responded by saying, "I would be honored if you would consider trying it on when you get back home." Jacob returned the smile and nodded his head in agreement.

Derek and Wallace kept their sunglasses firmly in place on their faces as Michael placed a steady hand on each of their shoulders. He looked both of them in the eye, through the dark mirrored lenses, and stated that... *the choice was theirs to make.*

The two boys were conscious of the encouragement in Michael's voice and briefly noticed the warmth of his smile. Michael nodded to them, reassured that a glimmer of hope had gotten through.

Circling the fire one last time, Michael sent up a silent prayer to the heavens. After he had finished, he returned to the empty seat across from his enemy.

Sitting quietly while listening to the crackling fire, the group of nine were deep in thought when Max stood up and walked over to Stryker. The raindrop, hanging from the leather cord, was held firmly in his hand when Max brought the heel of his boot down hard on the toe of the man in black. He pressed down further, twisting his foot, while pushing off with all of his weight. Stryker grimaced and watched Max returned to his seat on the log.

"It looks like our boy... thinks he's a man!" Stryker responded, sarcastically.

Max took another look at his raindrop and stood back up. There was one more task to accomplish. He squatted down by the fire and reached his fingers into the flames, pulling out seven glowing embers. He carried them over to Michael and opened his hands. Michael took a deep breath and slowly exhaled, blowing across the embers, cooling them off. After they were turned into small pieces of petrified wood, Max walked around the circle to hand a piece to each of his friends. Pausing in front of them, he repeated two words... "Always remember."

On his way back to his seat on the log, he walked past Stryker. Stopping to face him, he opened his hands and held them up for the steely gray eyes to inspect.

"See? Not a problem. Always remember!"

Max sat back down to quietly bask in the light of redemption.

As the fire started dying down, the minds of the seven young people were flooded with memories, beginning with their very first one from childhood.

Colorful balloons at a cousin's birthday party... a new puppy on Christmas morning... fireworks on the 4th of July... a scary ride at an amusement park... swimming lessons... angry words followed by a slamming door... a trip to the Grand Canyon...

On this night, their entire lives were being lived out within their memories. Visually, playing out like a reel of film in a movie theater, the phenomenon occurred within a matter of seconds, but was somehow revealed in slow motion. It was unexplainable.

When it came time for the journey from Mystic Woods to begin... only to end up at the present campfire... emotions seemed especially heightened.

The fork in the trail... the path less traveled... the music floating on the breeze in the forest... the journey itself! There were so many thoughts and unanswered questions.

Booming thunder... crashing lightning! Waves, on a rocky shoreline... an eagle's cry on the wind... bagpipes... laughter... a roaring fire... the beating of a drum...

Before the experience became more than they could handle, the seven were pulled away by the cadence and rhythm of the drum... as it was beginning to mimic the sound of the human heartbeat...

Stryker was the first to speak, breaking the spell...

Children of the night, dance in the dark. Celebrate this life and party like rock stars! LIVE, like there's no tomorrow. Think for yourselves. Don't be blinded by the light... step boldly into the night! Wrap that black velvet cloak about you and go wherever the road takes you. Do what YOU want to do! It's your choice... it's all up to you... seize the day... live for the moment! Let me show you the way. Follow me... this world is your playground... get everything you can from it! Flying high, grab the brass ring!

Make things happen for yourselves and take care of number one! I can show you the way... I'm your friend... you can trust me...

A shadow fell over his sinister face as he bowed before them.

Michael had the final say...

Life is about choices. Right and wrong... good and evil... light and darkness.

Do not be deceived... you must make a choice... the choice is yours, to make.

There is a book. A book worth reading... words worth contemplating.

Man cannot dismiss that which he has yet to consider.

There is a book. A book worth reading...

There was a man. A simple man. A strong man. A man of conviction. A kind man.

A carpenter...

He walked in the light...

He is the Light. He speaks the truth... He is the Way...He is the Truth... He is the Life...

He paid the price and offers a gift. The gift is free and is His to give...

There is a book. A book worth reading.

Embrace the truth... walk in the light.

Shadow has no place here... darkness must flee... and we all must choose.

There is a book. A book worth reading...

When the last words were spoken... the drumbeat stopped.

All was silent...

and everything went black.

DÉJÀ VU?

"...Reveille?" yawned Max as he rubbed his eyes.

"Is that a harmonica??" whispered a confused Jake.

Thaddeus was walking around and over the groggy teenagers, while playing a slow, folk-like version of *Reveille* on his juice harp. With the rushing water flowing in Trapper's Creek, it was the perfect accompaniment to the mountaineer's wakeup call.

Forty minutes earlier...

The five-minute warning had been given for the last leg of the journey to begin. Miss Trent had been heading to the water's edge to wash her hands, when she twisted her ankle. She slipped on a mossy rock and could barely hobble, let alone hike down the trail.

Thaddeus decided that the group should stay a little longer and take a nap in the shade, read quietly, bask in the sun or sketch a picture of their surroundings, while Miss Trent's ankle was tended to.

Mrs. Welch, a part-time nurse as well as a teacher, assisted Naomi with her injury. The foot was submerged in the ice-cold creek to help lessen some of the inflammation. After soaking the ankle, Nurse Welch gently massaged some natural herbal ointment into the affected area. Thankfully, the emergency medical kit that accompanied all outings, also included an elastic bandage. Miss Trent's injured foot would definitely need some added support, if she was going to make it back down the mountain to the lodge that afternoon.

After Naomi received an over-the-counter anti-inflammatory, it was Nurse Welch's recommendation that the foot be elevated for at least thirty minutes, to let the medication take effect. The trip down would have to be delayed. There was no getting around it.

Mr. Sherman and Thaddeus agreed that extending their stay at Trapper's Creek was a must. Most of the students were exhausted from the day's adventure and they welcomed the additional rest and relaxation. They were only too happy, to once again, dump their daypacks back on the ground, remove their boots, and stretch their tired feet.

Let's face it, teenagers are gifted at catching extra sleep wherever and whenever possible, and laying down in the wilderness for a powernap was right-up their alley. If they were to find sleep impossible, they were encouraged to keep the peace by refraining from talking.

Within five minutes, most of the weary teens were sawing logs and dreaming dreams...

"Ok, everybody! Time to wake up and get moving! Miss Trent is feeling like she can make it back down, so we're going to head that way!"

When it came to wrangling young people, Mr. Sherman was a great motivator, especially when it included crabby sleepy ones. Noticing that Max and Jake seemed to be hesitating, he thought that they must have slept really hard.

Walking towards them, he said, "Hey, guys, you're looking a bit sluggish. Is everything Ok?"

Jacob responded, "Yeah, I think my daypack/pillow might have cut the circulation off to my brain. Weird dreams."

"Same here," echoed Max.

"Ok... well, hustle up because you don't want to be left behind."

Max and Jake made eye contact for a brief moment, exchanging unspoken thoughts, as they laced up their boots. There was no time for conversation, so they grabbed their packs and lined up on the trail.

Shayne, also struggling with her current surroundings, reached for the cord hanging around her neck, only to realize that it wasn't there. When she leaned down to look in her pack for it, her sunglasses fell from the top of her head, landing on the ground. Startled, she stared at them for a minute before picking them up. It didn't make sense...

Trying to justify the puzzle forming in his mind, Wallace immediately jumped into action. He was certain there was a reasonable scientific explanation for what may or may not have occurred, and he was determined to discover it. In the meantime, he stuffed his dirty socks, a candy wrapper, and a half-eaten cookie into his daypack.

Daisy and Claire, avoiding eye contact with everyone around them, put all thoughts aside as they prepared to leave the creek.

Feeling angry and distrustful, Derek made sure that his sunglasses were situated firmly on his face, before finding his place in line. There was no time for thinking, and that was fine with him. Thinking, just seemed to make things more confusing.

The trip down from Trapper's Creek to Mystic Woods seemed way too familiar to seven of the hikers. With their senses on high alert, their eyes darted back and forth, scanning the trail. Each step brought them closer and closer to that pivotal moment where earlier, everything had changed. Or had it?

As they approached the darkened section of the trail within the magical forest, seven pairs of ears were intently listening for the sound of a wooden flute. And when a fellow student walking in front of Max attempted to speak, the boy was given a sharp slap on the back.

"HUSH!!" snapped Max, stopping in his tracks.

As he stared off into the forest, the young man in front of him spun around and balled up his fist.

"WAIT! I'm sorry... I really am! I thought I heard something and I just reacted! I am truly, very sorry." Max grabbed the boy, spun him back around and patted him gently on the back.

"So sorry..."

The fact of the matter was... there was no music floating on the breeze, coming from a wooden flute, and it didn't take long for the seven jumpy individuals to realize it. When they neared the place in the trail where they believed the path branched off, their resolve was tested. An overgrown tangle of foliage appeared to be camouflaging a fork in the trail, and a shiver ran down their spines. Once past the proverbial exit mark, they tried to convince themselves that it really wasn't there. They must have been imagining things. It had to be a crazy dream!

"You'd think I'd been sipping moonshine," said Wallace, under his breath.

"What did you just say, Wallace?" asked Mr. Sherman.

"Uh... I said... my boots could use a good shoeshine, Sir. They're very dusty!"

"That's what I thought you said," replied the skeptical counselor.

The rest of the trip down the mountain was quiet and uneventful. Everyone was too tired to talk, and they just wanted to get back to their cabins to freshen up.

Miss Trent did extraordinarily well on the hike down the mountain. Wallace even thought that she might have had a sip or two of moonshine from her "water bottle!" He wasn't beyond believing that the counselors had treated themselves to adult beverages over the past week. After all, they were of age, and they had to put up with a bunch of hormonal teenagers. More power to them!

When they rounded that last bend in the trail, and Soaring Eagle Lodge came into view, a riotous cheer went up! A second cheer followed when Mr. Sherman granted them exactly one hour to cool off, shower, reorganize, and get ready for dinner. The only condition was... *they had to bring a hardy appetite with them!*

With that said, they gladly dispersed, and raced towards the cabins.

An hour later, Cookie hammered away on the triangle, signaling that dinner was ready, and the hungry, freshly showered, sunburned bunch of campers, were eager to oblige him.

Par for the course, a shoving match ensued between the boys as they jockeyed for position at the front of the line. The girls, on the other hand, were polite enough and smart enough to step out of their way, although, one of the "unlucky ones" did take an elbow to the ribs... and she reacted by hollering, "Savages!!"

Thaddeus walked by just in time to say something to the boys about gentlemanly behavior. Apologies followed and order was restored.

"All-righty-rooney!" cried the exuberant cook. "I've got two black angus steaks here with names on em! Would Maxwell Darington & Claire Mathews please come to the front of the line to accept these fine cuts of beef?!"

With big grins on their faces, Max and Claire were more than happy to receive their reward. Thaddeus, standing next to them, said, "And after you two have enjoyed your meal, I'll take you to Inspiration Aspen, so you can leave your mark on the tree before it gets too dark." The pair nodded their heads and thanked their host.

A special table for two, complete with white tablecloth and matching cloth napkins, was set near the rock fireplace. A jar of wildflowers rested in the middle of the table, and two tall glasses of ice were waiting to be filled with their favorite soda.

While they were eating their meal, Claire shyly said to her dinner partner, "Can I ask you a question, Max? I mean, did you happen to...maybe... see something out of the ordinary... I mean... when we... well... I mean..." She kept her eyes on her plate as her sentence trailed off, "Oh, never mind..."

"Claire, I think I know what you want to say... but... well..."

Seeing Miss Trent beelining for their table, Max continued by whispering, "Oh, just forget it."

The limping counselor arrived at their table, abruptly interrupting their dinner conversation.

"Hey there you two lucky bird watchers! Are you enjoying the fruits of your labor this evening? This all looks very swanky! Say, could you two just lean together so I can take a picture to capture the moment?"

She shoved their chairs towards one another, making a scraping sound that put fingernails on a chalkboard to shame. All eyes in the dining area turned towards the trio. Claire turned bright red, just as the *bold photographer* snapped the picture. The flash from the camera temporarily blinded the two diners and before they could recover, Miss Trent had already moved on to the next table.

"Well, that was memorable!" exclaimed Max, while Claire just giggled awkwardly.

Hamburgers, hotdogs, potato chips and fresh fruit were on the menu for the rest of the crowd, and noisy chatter filled the lodge as stories were swapped over the festive meal. When Miss Trent had finished *capturing the moment* at all of the tables, she helped herself to a tray full of food. Hobbling over to Mr. Sherman's table, she wiggled her way down onto the bench, facing her favorite colleague, by placing herself between Daisy and Wallace.

"Don't these burgers & dogs look wonderful?! And the fruit? Delicious! We are so lucky to have such a great chef here at Soaring Eagle! And isn't this just the most beautiful lodge you've ever seen?! The carvings... the rock fireplace... the paintings... the photographs... well... just... everything?!"

Wallace, with a straight face, interrupted her by saying, "I like steak better."

With dinner and dessert behind them, Claire and Max were happy to put the photo session and Miss Trent's rambling dialog in their rearview mirror. Together, they stepped away from the table and went looking for Thaddeus. They found him standing inside the door of the lodge, talking and laughing with their bus driver, Mr. Graves. They could tell that the two men were good friends. When Thaddeus saw Max and Claire approaching them, he shook hands with his old comrade and excused himself from their conversation.

"Are you two ready to go carve your names in that tree?" They nodded their heads. "Then let's get going!"

"Is it very far from the lodge?" asked Claire.

"No, not far at all, young lady. It's just a hop, skip and a jump from here."

"Great," added Max. "Speaking for myself, I'm pretty tired of walking."

Thaddeus chuckled and Claire just smiled, as they walked the short distance to the aspen tree.

"WHOA! That tree is huge!!" cried Max, and Claire echoed his sentiment by stating, "WHOA... is RIGHT!!"

Thaddeus handed them each a pocket knife and instructed the pair on proper handling and appropriate carving.

"I suggest that you each choose a side of the tree to work on... and by all means, do the tree proud! Ten years from now you may come back to revisit it... to remember..."

On opposite sides of the aspen, they both sucked in their breath.

Remember?! THAT'S an interesting choice of words!

Returning his attention to the task at hand, Maxwell carved his first initial and last name, along with the date, on his side of the aspen. As an afterthought, he added a coiled snake with opened mouth and sharp fangs.

Claire carved her full name, the date... and a dove suspended within a raindrop. When they were finished, they circled the tree to admire each other's handiwork. The moment Max saw the dove and Claire saw the snake, they raced around the tree and collided with one another. Reaching out, they grasped each other's forearms and locked eyes. No words were needed.

Thaddeus began whistling a tune and walking back towards the lodge. With the pied piper leading the way, they dropped their hands to their sides, turned away from each other, and silently followed after him.

CAMPFIRE SONGS

Thaddeus found Derek and Mr. Sherman tending the fire in the firepit down by the lake.

"Thank you, boys, for getting the fire started without me. I really do appreciate your help. If you don't mind watching it for a few more minutes, I'm going to run to my cabin and grab my guitar and instruments for tonight. I won't be long."

"We don't mind at all. Derek and I can stay here and watch over it until you get back." Dax reached out and affectionately gripped Derek's shoulder. "Derek is the one who deserves all the credit for tonight's fire though. He had it built and burning before I even got here."

Not one to receive compliments, Derek shrugged his shoulders and said, "It was no big deal."

"Well, my boy, if I'd known you had a gift for fire building, I'd have recruited you at the beginning of the week! You know, not everyone has the skill needed when it comes to building fires."

Whistling a tune and kicking up a cloud of dust in his wake, Thaddeus smiled as he marched off in the direction of his cabin.

The evening was turning out to be a chilly one and extra sweatshirts were a must. Claire and Max had gone straight back to their cabins to get ready for the final campfire, and hadn't had the opportunity to talk to anyone. Max was eager to talk to Jake and to the others, if time allowed, but Claire was still trying to understand what had transpired at Inspiration Aspen. It certainly wasn't a coincidence that the carvings in the tree triggered a similar reaction, and at some point, she and Max would need to talk about it. Claire just needed time to figure out how to broach the subject.

Once back in her cabin, Claire thought about talking to Shayne, but when she saw the brooding girl sitting on her bunk with her sunglasses on, she decided that now was not the time. It would have to be later.

Miss Trent was cleaning her pith helmet with a soft cloth when Claire stepped past her. Shayne looked up at Claire and said, "She's putting the shine on it for Dax... I mean, for Mr. Sherman, and I'm guessing that he's slapping on some cologne for Naomi... I mean, Miss Trent. I think the lack of oxygen here in high country has started something."

Miss Trent replied, "Well, young lady, when you're older I believe you'll meet someone worth polishing your helmet over."

"I think you should plant some flowers in your helmet and put it on Mr. Sherman's desk as a souvenir... to remember our trip!" smirked Shayne.

"Why... that's a wonderful idea! I think I'll do just that! Thanks for the tip, Shayne!" said the lovestruck counselor as she continued cleaning and polishing her prized headgear.

"Oh, brother..." whispered the sarcastic girl with the sunglasses on.

On the way to the fire, several girls had linked arms and were scissoring their feet to the right and then the left, laughing, while trying not to trip each other in the process. The boys, on the other hand, were dragging their feet and trying to trip each other and were purposefully kicking up clouds of dust, just to annoy the girls.

The campfire was roaring away when the last of the senior class arrived at the lake. As the students gathered around the crackling fire, Mr. Sherman scanned the crowd to see if anyone was missing.

"Hey... where's Wallace?!"

"I'M COMING, MR. SHERMAN!!" hollered Wallace on the run. "I WAS ASLEEP... and no one woke me up!" He skidded to a halt in front of his counselor.

Wallace's hair was sticking up in the back, and a line of drool running from the corner of his mouth to his chin, had dried up on his face.

"Better late than never, Mr. Sherman!"

"DEBATABLE!" piped up someone from around the fire.

"Find a spot, Wallace, and try to stay awake."

Wallace glanced around the fire, searching for a place to land. There were logs for sitting on around the firepit, but they all seemed to have been taken. The remainder of his classmates stood shoulder to shoulder behind those who were lucky enough to find a seat. He'd just have to shove his way in between a few of them, somehow.

When Daisy and Claire felt a hand on each of their shoulders, they turned and looked up at Wallace. With a grin, he pushed them apart and plopped down on the log between them.

"Evening, ladies!" he said with grand bravado.

"Great..." stated Daisy, as she rolled her eyes up towards the dark night sky.

Wallace ran his hands through his hair, and rubbed at the dried-up drool on his chin with the sleeve of his sweatshirt. Claire just stared at her boots and tried to make herself as small as possible.

The sound of the all too familiar bagpipes, brought everyone's attention to the Scotch-Irish Rooster's timely arrival. Huffing and puffing and playing for all he was worth, Thaddeus stepped into the light of the fire, causing laughter to erupt.

Their illustrious host was wearing a kilt on the bottom half, a flannel shirt on the top half, an Indian headdress on his head, and hippie beads around his neck. He had red and black warpaint on one cheek, and a purple and green peace sign on the other. His guitar hung from its strap across his back, and he had a pink furry slipper on one foot, with a black leather dress shoe on the other. His moustache was waxed and he wore no socks. His legs were hairy.

When he was finished playing the bagpipes, Thaddeus set them down near a pine tree and swung his guitar around in front of him.

"Kum-bai-yah, my peeps...Kum-bai-yah... Kum-bai-yah, my peeps... Kum-bai-yah..."

When he had finished singing the song, a round of applause broke forth from the crowd and Thaddeus took a bow... and then another... and another... and another...

Next, he pulled his harmonica from his pocket and played a lively Irish tune. Several folk songs followed, accompanied by the guitar. With feet stomping and hands clapping, the overall mood was upbeat and energizing.

When a break from performing was needed, Thaddeus set his

instrument down and grabbed the person nearest to him. Pushing his *backup entertainment* out front and center, after a formal introduction, he announced that he or she would be singing a song, telling a joke, reciting a poem or sharing a ghost story. From there, that lucky person would have to improvise. It soon became a crowd favorite as the *victims* were proving to be good sports about it.

In the end, Miss Trent won the proverbial prize. When she was pulled from the group and thrust into the spotlight, Thaddeus proudly announced that Miss Trent would be reciting a poem, never heard before, fresh from the African tundra!

Naomi Trent, standing straight and tall, adjusted her khaki jacket, tipped her pith helmet back, and proceeded to say... "Fresh from the African tundra... a poem... never heard before! And it goes something like this..."

There once was a lion, named Hal... who was lonely and longed for a pal... so he fluffed up his mane... and his whiskers, the same... and abruptly he ran into Al! Well... Al was not Clarisse... nor Cher... nor Lil... nor Patrice! Yes, Al was just Al... not the hoped-for pal... for Hal really wanted Marlise! Or Betty... or Marietta... or Fredricka... or June... or Rosa Maria... or Marianna... or Nell... or Linda Lou... or Madge... or Trixie... or Annie Moon... or Liza... or Tina... or...

"THANK YOU, Miss Trent!! Thank you for that lovely rendition... fresh from Africa!"

Thaddeus, trying to keep a straight face, clapped enthusiastically while the students, laughing so hard, almost fell off of the logs that they were sitting on. Needless to say, the evening was turning out to be quite entertaining.

Things quieted down, when suddenly, Running Deer appeared from the shadows wearing warpaint on his serious, warrior's face. He walked slowly around the firepit staring deeply into the eyes of every teenager there. After circling around the fire twice, he had gained their full attention. With great care and dramatic flair, he began reciting an old Indian tale from long ago. Halfway through, he had the majority of them quaking in their hiking boots.

The story began with vicious gray wolves stalking human prey who were caught unaware, while sleeping beneath the stars. It continued by telling of giant grizzlies overtaking predators, deep in the woods. The mighty bison followed after, as they thundered across the prairie, crushing everything in their path. The story also spoke of the power of the wind and its ability to direct the flight of the majestic eagle. With small creatures clasped in their claws, the cries in the night were soul shattering. He ended the tale with the light of the moon shining down to reveal all things lurking within the dark shadows of the night...

All eyes were intensely riveted on Running Deer... as he slowly crept backwards into the trees, disappearing into the shadows...

"And on that note, folks, I'd like to share one last song before we all hit the hay!" said a cheerful, Thaddeus.

Strumming a few cords, he sat down on a log with his guitar resting comfortably on his lap.

"Each year, I like to write a special song for the class. I work on it all week long and it's what I refer to as *my* homework. While you're all writing in journals, taking snapshots, and collecting mementos, I'm working on your song... and this year, it goes something like this..."

The sound coming from Thaddeus' old beat-up guitar was so beautiful and unexpected, especially to Jacob, Daisy, Max, Derek, Claire, Shayne and Wallace. The arrangement he was playing had a mesmerizing effect on them, as it wasn't the first time that they had heard it. A wooden flute playing mysteriously in the forest, echoed within the memory of a mutual journey, and Thaddeus and his guitar had their full attention.

All ears were listening carefully when the lyrics to the song were delivered, during which seven of the students were finding themselves barely able to breathe...

When you see a fork in a well-worn path... the choice is up to you. Are you lured away, do you take a left... or to the path stay true?

On a dark starry night, when the moon is full... the choice is up to you. Are you lulled by the sound of the underground... or to the path still stay true?

When you see a fork in a well-worn path... the choice is up to you. When the light shines bright in the dark of night... it's there to guide you through.

When the light shines bright... in the dark of night... the light brings comfort too. In the dark of night... when it shines so bright... it's there... for me and you.

When you see that fork... from the well-worn path... the choice is up to you. Are you lured away... are you lulled by the sound... or to the path stay true?

Will the true light take you through? Will it guide and comfort too? The choice is up to you... the choice is up to you...

When the song ended, Thaddeus Barron stood up and simply said, "Pleasant dreams."

Walking away from the campfire, he continued to whistle the mysterious tune...

THE TASK AT HAND

Daisy and Wallace were on a mission. They walked straight from the fire to their cabins. Digging through their duffle bags, they searched for the raindrop necklaces that had been given to them at the flower festival. Once located, they immediately placed them over their heads and around their necks. Deep sighs expelled the pent-up fear that began plaguing them when the campfire ended.

Thaddeus' song had stirred up mixed emotions within the seven anxious teenagers. The hornet's nest had been poked with a stick and their minds were left buzzing. Those that were focusing on their sunglasses, were certainly not focusing on the raindrop necklaces.

Daisy and Wallace had different thoughts when it came to their sunshades. Wallace also checked his duffle bag to see if his sunglasses were still there. He wasn't really sure if he wanted to keep them. He considered selling them to the pawn shop back in Chloe. He'd have to think about it.

Daisy knew exactly what she was going to do next. Grabbing

her sunglasses from her daypack, she walked boldly towards the door. When asked where she was going, she hollered back over her shoulder, "Just to the bathroom... I'll be right back!"

The determined girl veered to the right, just before reaching the bathhouse. Walking as far as she felt comfortable into the darkened woods, she went until she was far enough from sight. Retrieving a small flashlight from her pocket, she flipped it on. When she stumbled upon a very large upturned tree root, she began digging a hole beneath it with her bare hands. Next, she stuffed the sunglasses down in the hole as far as she possibly could, and covered them up with the loose dirt. She searched for rocks, pine straw, and any debris nearby, to pile on top of it. When she was satisfied with her work, she walked back to the bathhouse to scrub the dirt from her hands. Before anyone could suspect a thing, she was back in the cabin, snug in her sleeping bag, with the mysterious music still echoing through her mind.

Derek knew that he'd left his necklace somewhere at home. He believed it was in the bottom drawer of his dresser, but he wasn't sure. He planned on looking for it when he got back to the house, just to see if it was something to consider keeping.

The sunglasses were with him though and he put them back on. When his fingers came in contact with the smooth plastic frame, a nervous energy surged through him, followed by an eerie calm. It reminded him of the night when fog had settled like a blanket over Pale Moon Lake around midnight. Contemplating his future, he wasn't sure if he was ready to give up his shades quite yet.

Jacob, upon entering his cabin, took his sunglasses off and shoved them to the bottom of his duffle bag. In his mind, he could see the raindrop attached to the leather cord, hanging from the rearview mirror in his pickup truck back home. He knew that it wouldn't be hanging there for long, because his plan was to hang it around his neck and leave it there until the leather cord was worn down thin enough to break. Then, he'd buy another cord and restring it. He truly believed it would be in his best interest to do so. The sunglasses, on the other hand, he'd think about later.

Max devised his own plan. He feigned a coughing fit and excused himself so he could step outside to clear his lungs with some cold mountain air. Before leaving the cabin, he shoved his sunglasses into his pants pocket. He didn't feel the need to walk too far into the woods to accomplish his goal. He decided he'd just head back towards the lake. Once there, he pulled the evil glasses from his pocket, snapped them in half, and tossed them on top of the smoldering embers in the campfire. He watched them melt as demonic laughter and sinister screeching arose from the pit.

After shouting, "GOOD RIDDANCE!" Max shivered, and jogged quickly back to his cabin.

Shayne was the last one with a decision to make and she knew exactly what she had to do. When the lights went out, she patiently waited to hear Miss Trent's whiffling snore. Their fearless leader was predictably quick to enter dreamland, and once there, Shayne would give her a solid ten minutes more, to fall deeply into snooze mode.

Sneaking out of the cabin was easy for Shayne. She'd had plenty of practice at home under her parents' *watchful eyes!* With her sunglasses in one hand and a small flashlight in the other, she made her move towards the door.

Claire sat up on her bunk and made eye contact with the rule breaker, and Shayne froze in her tracks, not sure if Minnie was going to sound the alarm or not. Claire nodded her head in silent approval, and waved Shayne towards the door.

Shayne kept to the shadows and headed for the lake. She found a heavy rock and pulled a hairband from her pocket. Tightly binding the sunglasses to the stone, she made sure that they would not come apart. She removed her boots, socks and pants, and waded out into the lake up to her midthighs. With all of the strength she possessed, she hurled the bundled shades as far out over the water as possible. When she heard the splash, she said, "TAKE THAT!!"

She made her way back onto the shore and used her hands to wipe some of the water from her legs. When she was fully dressed, she stood and looked out over the dark lake. The water seemed to be bubbling and gasping in the area where the rock had been thrown, reminding Shayne of snake infested waters. A shiver ran down her spine.

She ran as fast as she could with her heart thumping wildly. When she neared the cabin, she stopped and leaned up against a tree to catch her breath. The cabin door squeaked slightly when she reentered, but Miss Trent never missed a beat with her continuous snoring.

This time, it was Shayne who nodded at Claire, acknowledging that the mission had been accomplished.

FOREVER...

Sleep did not come easy that last night at camp for the four boys and three girls. They tossed and turned and relived the past week, while a haunting song played quietly in their minds...

When you see a fork in a well-worn path... the choice is up to you...

How in the world did Thaddeus come up with THAT song? Was it all just a dream? Who were those two guys from the Flower Festival? Why did they come to Chloe? Why did the sunglasses feel sleek and cool one moment... and hot and dangerous the next? What is the significance of the raindrop? How come the necklace feels like shelter in a storm? Safety, in time of peril. What does it all mean?

If there really is a choice to be made... then where do I stand?

So many thoughts. They hadn't yet found the moment, nor had the courage to talk amongst each other about what may or may not have happened on the mountain. It was all still so fresh and unsettling, and there were too many unanswered questions.

Mentally, reliving the journey was exhausting. All that had been seen... all that had been experienced... all of the visions and messages... it was all, too much.

When they could no longer battle the images running through their minds, they gave up the fight and fell into a deep, deep sleep...

The sky was flat, lifeless, and charcoal gray. There were no clouds. It was a heavily laden blank canvas, bearing down on those beneath it.

Two opposing figures, facing one another from across a great divide, were standing on the edge. The ground leading up to the cliff on the left was rocky and barren. Nothing grew there. On the right, tall grass reached midcalf, to the man standing in it.

The man on the left, dressed in black, stared with fierce arrogance at the man on the right dressed in white. From a distance, it was difficult to distinguish their facial features.

Eyes were held captive by the chasm before them. The great abyss... the indescribable darkness that separated them... it was ominous and palpable. Bottomless. No light could penetrate its foreboding presence.

Fingers of fear shook the atmosphere, tightening its grip around the throat of every victim, depriving oxygen from entering the lungs. Soul shaking fear was sheathed in utter darkness.

There was no sound. Not even the clicking of the reel spinning when the silent film played. The absence of sound was deafening. There were no words to fully describe that which was transpiring...

Stillness...

... but the canvas was about to change.

Like a camera snapping photos in rapid succession, with each image captured, the two subjects grew closer and closer, revealing their identities. When the grass began to sway as the wind swept across the canvas, tension began to build.

What began as a soft humming noise floating on the breeze, soon evolved into a rhythmic thrumming, like fingers bouncing off a drum. What came next was unforeseen...

With a stroke from the artist's brush, the flat gray backdrop was infused with new life, and a powerful whirring sound was heard traveling across the now heavenly swath of blue.

In the distance, approaching from the right, were thousands upon thousands of white doves, flying across the open sky. The flowing current that followed them energized the air, bringing life giving oxygen. Trees, flowers, greenery, foliage... suddenly filled in the landscape below to the right.

The left side of the canvas remained stark gray and barren. An appropriate setting for the man in black. Standing stone still, steadily staring at the man in white, he on the left, never looked up to the heavenly flock flying overhead.

The man in white lifted his hands and eyes toward the heavens as peace and light shone forth from his countenance.

As the white birds drew near, bright light burst forth from above, and gold dust cascaded off the wings of the heaven-sent creatures. When the rays of light touched the golden particles, joy and forgiveness straight from heaven, rained down...

The one clothed in white, with hands lifted high, sifted the golden light through his fingers...

The one in black turned from the man in white and stared straight through me. With eyes as black as the abyss before him, he reached for his sunglasses, and covered up the windows to his tortured soul. Turning away from me, he willingly stepped off the edge... and was swallowed up by utter darkness.

Jacob... Wallace... Shayne... Derek... Maxwell... Daisy... and Claire, sat bolt upright in their bunks at the exact same moment in time. With hearts beating rapidly, the following were the first thoughts to enter each of their minds...

Jacob... *I'm going out in the boat and going fishing with Gramps, as soon as I get back home! We have things to talk about. Important things!*

Wallace... *Forget college... I'm joining the military!*

Shayne... *How much wood, would a woodchuck chuck, if a woodchuck could chuck wood? I'm thinking that it really doesn't matter! Maybe, I should go to college? Do something worthwhile with my life...*

Derek... *I'm going to find Dean and beat him within an inch of his life, and then I'm going to hug him and tell him a story about a camping trip in the mountains...*

Maxwell... *I'm building that boat! I'm going to sail it around the world! I'm going to find purpose in this life of mine!*

Daisy... *After college I'm going to write a book. I need to help people who struggle with rough beginnings. I want to help them find their happy ending!*

Claire... *I'm going to have to cut Dr. Morton Mathews' hair short, because he's going to be very hot in the Middle East. We're joining the Peace Corps...*

Before the seven could move on to second thoughts, the first rays of sunlight shot through their cabin windows.

Jacob saw the golden shimmering dust floating in the air. In stunned silence, he held his breath and watched it drift down to land on the boots by his bunk.

Wallace put his hand out and watched it sift through his fingers. His mouth was hanging open and his hair was sticking up.

Shayne shook her head from side to side, and stared at the bright golden particles floating in the air. She was trying extra hard to understand what she was seeing.

Derek picked up the sunglasses sitting on the windowsill beside his bunk. He watched the gold dust slide right off of them, eventually landing on the cabin floor. His face was unreadable.

Max looked down at his sleeping bag and patted the top of it with his hand. A cloud of sparkling gold puffed upwards into the air. *Wow!*

Daisy was awestruck. She laid her head back down on her pillow and looked up at the ceiling. She watched the minute specks dance above her, captured within the rays of light. She closed her eyes and imagined them covering the contours of her face.

Claire reached out her hand and slowly ran it across the top post of the upper bunk. Millions and millions of tiny golden particles coated her hand and shimmered down towards the floor... and the smile on her face... was as bright as the morning sun.

JOHN 3:16 For God so loved the world that He gave His only begotten Son, that whosoever believes in Him should not perish but have everlasting life.

EPILOGUE

Five years later...

The dirt covered cargo truck left a cloud of dust in its wake as it bounced along the rock-strewn road. The remote village only received deliveries once a month, and everyone eagerly ran to see what civilization had in store for them this time.

Claire walked up to the delivery truck as boxes of food, medical supplies, cleaning agents, tools, and personal hygiene products were being unloaded. She was happy to see that most of what had been ordered, appeared to be included in the load.

"Hi, Chauncy! Did you bring any word from home? Maybe a letter or two?" asked the confident young woman.

"You know it, Claire! Your family must miss you terribly. They never fail to write. You also have a package this time... addressed from... 'Soaring Eagle Lodge?'" he handed the small box to the surprised Peace Corp worker.

"Wow! It's from Thaddeus Barron. I wonder how he found me? Anyway, thank you Chauncy." Claire accepted the package and walked to her tent cabin to open the box in privacy.

Within the same month, six more packages were delivered...

2nd Lieutenant Wallace Kramer was stationed in Japan when a package with his name on it arrived at the military base.

"NO WAY! How did the Scotch-Irish Rooster find me?!"

A grin stretched from ear to ear, as he excused himself to go open the box in the privacy of his office.

Jacob never left Chloe. When his grandfather passed away suddenly, just one year after he had graduated from high school, Jake knew that he would stay at the lake house and keep Henry's memory alive. College wasn't for him. He preferred working with his hands and when Joseph, a local home builder, asked him to join his crew, Jake accepted.

He and Henry had an entire year to fish, talk about the past, contemplate the future, and just live life surrounded by the mountains that they loved. Jacob would always cherish that precious gift of time that had been given to them.

One day, after arriving home from work, he was surprised to see a package sitting at his back door. When he saw who it was from, he was doubly surprised.

"What in the world could this be?"

He carried the box inside and set it on the kitchen table. He decided to shower off the layer of dirt and sawdust from the workday, before seeing what the packaged contained...

Shayne gave college a try, but found that it was more work than she was willing to exert. After one semester, she opted for beauty school. It would take less time to accomplish the end result, and she really loved her hair. The thought of coming up with unique styles, and possibly working with the Hollywood crowd, appealed to her.

The latest segment of *Tripping to Remember*, was being filmed in Washington State. A travel show, featuring a musical band of hippie's, visiting and performing at various National Parks in the United States, was proving popular with young rebels. Shayne, prior to filming, had interviewed for the Hair & Makeup Stylist position and was hired on the spot. They were filming at their fifth location when the package arrived.

"Huh! From Thaddeus Barron... Soaring Eagle Lodge? Did I leave something behind... what... five or so years ago?"

Shayne shrugged, tossed the box in her oversized tote and decided she'd open it later.

When Max sailed back into the marina, the owner of the Bait & Tackle shop met him at the dock. Max threw him the rope and climbed out of his boat. After securing his sailboat to the dock, he turned and thanked the man for his help.

"Say, Max, this came for you today."

A small package was placed in the hands of the young sailor.

"Seriously? Who gave this to you?" asked Max.

"Wiley, our UPS man. He delivered it this morning."

Max read the return address and stared out over the lake. Memories of a camping trip in the mountains came flooding back. He thanked the store owner and proceeded to walk to his SUV.

He was curious to see the package's contents, but thought he'd wait until he got back to the house before opening it.

Daisy had just finished proofreading the final chapter of her first book and was eager to pass it on to her editor. She was anxious to make her mark in the world of literature, and a self-help book focusing on children without parents, was her first attempt. College had been challenging, but also encouraging, and she could hardly wait to hear what the professionals had to say about her labor of love.

When a knock at the door of her apartment captured her attention, she was certain it was her favorite college roommate, Leslie. They were planning on catching dinner and a movie that night.

When she opened the door, she was surprised to see that no one was there, but before closing it, she noticed a small box sitting on the front step.

"Soaring Eagle Lodge? Where did you come from, little box?"

Daisy closed the door and proceeded to open it…

After hitchhiking around the country, trying to follow leads on his brother Dean's disappearance, Derek gave up and decided to stay in Los Angeles for a while. The last bit of information given to him by a private investigator, brought him to the southern California city. Although it seemed unlikely, he hoped he might cross paths with his older brother. Maybe he'd see him at a bus stop or at the beach one day.

He'd rented a small studio apartment in a rough part of town, and had been hired to tend bar at a nearby club. His plan was to work at night, while showing Dean's picture to as many people as possible. Working the late shift allowed him to continue searching for Dean during the day, and sleeping, would just have to take back burner.

Derek kept in touch with his mother, and he decided that she must have given Mr. Sherman his address. When a package was left at his apartment, from the old man that ran Soaring Eagle Lodge, he figured his high school counselor must have passed his whereabouts on to the guy.

When Derek opened the box, he was stunned to see what was in it...

Dear Derek,

Please accept this invitation to a private reunion at Soaring Eagle Lodge on New Year's Day. A select few have been chosen to return, and all travel expenses have been provided for via a donor requesting to remain anonymous. Room and board for one week will also be taken care of by said donor.

Please respond by December 1st... so that arrangements can be handled prior to travel. May God bless you and watch over you...

Sincerely,

Thaddeus Barron

In addition to the invitation, five items were included in the package. An aqua colored crystal... a solid gold aspen leaf... a black onyx stone... a tiny carved bird ... and a piece of petrified wood...from a memorable fire.

ACKNOWLEDGMENTS

I am grateful to God for John and Mary Lou Nystrom, the best parents a girl could ever hope for. Their love stretches well beyond this lifetime... and I am extremely blessed!

I'd like to send out an ocean-sized wave of gratitude to the following encouragers... John A. Nystrom, III, Lorrie Owens, Laura DuBose, Julie Freeman, Kristie Smith, Des Visser, Kim Bement, Trisha Conner, Jill Cunningham-Isley, Merideth Trovato and Brittney Wilkerson. There is a special place in my heart for each one of you.

To my beautiful and gifted niece, Mariah Nystrom Hayes, thank you for creating the cover for the book that I now hold in my hands. It's perfect!

To my family... David, Jared, Kaleb, Tyler, Lori, Amanda, Danielle, Brayden, Arabella, Patrick, Elijah, Robert, Little Brayden, Adalynne, Michaela, Flynn, Charles and Zane David. I love you all! You are forever in my heart, and again... I am so very blessed...

Most importantly, I give all the glory to my Lord and Savior, Jesus Christ. With my many faults and failings, He still loves me, and for this, I am eternally grateful...

You have a story.
We want to publish it.

Everyone has as a story to tell. It might be about something you know how to do, or what has happened in your life, or it may be a thrilling, or romantic, or intriguing, or heartwarming, or suspenseful story, starring a cast of characters that have been swimming around in your imagination.

And at Wyatt House Publishing, we can get your story onto the pages of a book just like the one you are holding in your hand. With professional interior design and a custom, professionally designed cover built just for you from the start, you can finally see your dream of being an author become reality. Then, you will see your book listed with retailers all over the world as people are able to buy your book from wherever they are and have it delivered to their home or their e-reader.

So what are you waiting for? This is your time.

visit us at

www.wyattpublishing.com

for details on how to get started becoming a
published author right away.

CPSIA information can be obtained
at www.ICGtesting.com
Printed in the USA
LVHW102053171022
730905LV00014B/516/J